GABRIEL'S
HORSES

GABRIEL'S HORSES

ALISON HART

PEACHTREE
ATLANTA

Published by
PEACHTREE PUBLISHERS
1700 Chattahoochee Avenue
Atlanta, Georgia 30318-2112
www.peachtree-online.com

Cover design by Loraine M. Joyner
Book design by Melanie McMahon Ives

Photo credits: pp. 152, 153, 154, 157, 161, courtesy of the Library of Congress; p.155, courtesy of the National Archives.

Printed in the United States of America
10 9 8 7 (hardcover)
10 9 8 7 6 5 4 3 2 1 (trade paperback)

Library of Congress Cataloging-in-Publication Data
Hart, Alison, 1950-
 Gabriel's horses / by Alison Hart. -- 1st ed.
  p. cm.
 Summary: In Kentucky, during the Civil War, the twelve-year-old slave, Gabriel, deals with a new cruel horse trainer, skirmishes with Confederate Soldiers, and pursues his dream of becoming a jockey.
 ISBN 13: 978-1-56145-398-6 / ISBN 10: 1-56145-398-6 (hardcover)
 ISBN 13: 978-1-56145-528-7 / ISBN 10: 1-56145-528-8 (trade paperback)
 [1. Horses--Fiction 2. Horse racing--Fiction. 3. Slavery--Fiction. 4. African Americans--Fiction. 5. Kentucky--History--Civil War, 1861-1865--Fiction. 6. United States--History--Civil War, 1861-1865--Fiction.] I. Title.
 PZ7.H256272Gab 2007
 [Fic]--dc22
                                        2006027697

To John L. Heatwole
Dedicated Historian, Writer, and Friend
—A. H.

CHAPTER ONE

The wrap goes like this, Gabriel," Pa tells me as he tugs the strip of rag around the horse's front leg. Stooped in the straw, I watch with hawk eyes. When Pa shows me something, I take note. Pa's the best horseman in Kentucky, and I aim to follow in his path. Besides, any fool knows that wrapping a racehorse's legs right is almost as important as riding him right.

"Keep the cotton wadding smooth," Pa adds, his forehead as furrowed and brown as a plowed field. "That's what protects the legs."

"Yes sir." I feel a warm tickle on my neck. Tenpenny's lipping my hair. "Get away, horse." I swat his muzzle playfully. Tenpenny is one of my favorites. Tomorrow, Master Giles is racing him in Lexington, and since I'm the lightest boy at Woodville Farm, I get to ride him the eight miles to the track.

At the thought of the journey, my belly churns. Sure, it ain't as exciting as jockeying Tenpenny in a race. That's Jackson's job. But this trip has got me plenty stirred up. I've never been to the big city of Lexington, or a racetrack either. Pa and Jackson have told me lots about both places, but that ain't the same as seeing with my own eyes.

Pa does the last wrap, then rises. "Finish grooming Penny. Make him shine the way Mister Giles likes. Then get ready to go. We head out after sunrise."

Using the softest bristles, I polish Tenpenny's gray flanks. Pa was born free, so he calls my master, Winston Giles, *mister.*

When I ask Ma why I have to call him master, she tells me it's 'cause I'm a slave chile. "I ain't no chile," I tell her. "I'm almost thirteen. A man."

Ma chuckles like I said something humorous. Then I smile, too, 'cause I like making Ma laugh. Since Mistress Jane, Master Giles's wife, caught the fever, there ain't been much joy in Ma's heart.

Standing back, I eye Tenpenny. He gleams as bright as Mistress Jane's silver tea tray. "You gonna win this race, Penny," I tell him as I stroke his silky neck.

Outside the stall, I hear Jackson whistling. Jackson is Woodville Farm's jockey. I swear he could ride a hog and win. All spring he's been teaching me how to ride like him. He says I've got the talent, too, so I practice every morning, hunching low on the horse's neck when we gallop the grassy track that winds through Master's fields.

"You got my horse ready, boy?" Jackson asks as he throws open the stall door. He's short and bandy-legged with a chest like a rain barrel. He's chewing on a stalk of hay. A checked cap slants low on his head like he's some Louisville dandy.

"Who wants to know?" I sass back.

Jackson cuffs me on the head. "You best show respect to the world's greatest jockey." Sticking his thumbs in his vest, he puffs out his chest.

"You ain't the world's greatest jockey," I say. "That's Abe Hawkins."

Many nights I've heard the story of how Abe Hawkins, an ex-slave from the South, beat the famous white jockey Gilpatrick in St. Louis. Last May Pa and Jackson traveled to St. Louis with Master Giles to see the races. Jackson said Hawkins even had his name "Abe" mentioned in an article in the *New York Herald*.

"When you beat Gilpatrick, then I'll show you some respect," I say, getting in one last jab.

Jackson chuckles at my joshing. Then his dark face grows serious. Like Pa, Jackson knows horses better than he knows himself. Thumbs still hooked in his vest, he walks around Tenpenny.

I follow behind like his shadow, trying to see with his smart eyes.

"Pa's got him wrapped for the walk to Lexington." I pat the colt's flank.

Jackson nods, his checked cap bobbing. "Colt looks fine, Gabriel," he says before leaving. "Should win tomorrow, I reckon."

I grin proud. When Jackson calls me Gabriel, I know he's mighty pleased.

"Be back in a jump," I tell Tenpenny, rubbing his nose. "I gotta say goodbye to the other horses."

I stop first at Captain Conrad's stall. He's another colt in training. I give his flank a quick pat and head to blind Patterson's stall. When I open the door, he pricks his ears. I hum "Camptown Races" to let him know it's me.

When Patterson was a colt, he won so many races that Pa lost count. Then one day he broke into the corn bin. Ate until he about bust. The horse doctor bled him, but the corn did something bad and Patterson started going blind. Now he bides his time in the pasture with the mares.

"I'll be gone for two days, but Jase or Tandy will turn you out," I tell the bay stallion. Jase and Tandy are the other grooms. Both are younger than me, but they care for the horses right fine.

Patterson whiffles my cheek. I shut the stall door and run out of the barn to say goodbye to the younguns. The morning sun's rising over Woodville Farm. Pastures surround the three red-brick horse barns, the supply shed, the carriage shed, and the hay barn. One brick barn is for Master Giles's Thoroughbreds. Pa's in charge of that barn, which is where I spend my time. A second barn is for the riding and carriage horses. Cato runs that one. Oliver, Cato's brother, is in charge of the last barn, the one that houses the mares and foals.

In the main pasture, Romance, Savannah, and Sympathy graze peacefully. When I whistle, the three fillies trot over, and I stroke their velvet muzzles. In the paddock next to them, Arrow and Daphne spar with their front hooves. I halloo, and they charge away, bucking.

My favorite colt, Aristo, is kept by himself 'cause he's so

wild. I climb the split-rail fence. Beyond the pastures, Master's cropland stretches from hill to hill. It's early summer and new plants shoot from the earth. In between the rows of corn and hemp, the field hands hunch low, hoeing weeds. Sometimes their sad songs reach my ears, and I thank Jesus I ain't in the fields.

When Aristo spies me straddling the rail, he prances over. His flaxen mane and tail billow like bloomers on the line, and his coat shines as red and glorious as this morning's sun. Tossing his head, he nips at my pants leg.

I laugh. "'Risto, you think you some fierce critter. But I know you ain't."

When the colt swings close, I spring onto his back. Twining my fingers through his mane, I squeeze my calves against his sides. He leaps in the air and takes off across the pasture. His stride lengthens into a gallop. I dig my bare heels into his ribs, urging him on. The dewy air slaps my face, and gnats catch in my teeth.

Mimicking Jackson, I burrow my fingers in the colt's mane and lean low on his neck. He wheels at the far corner, races back, and skids to a halt near the willow on the other side of the fence.

I raise one fist and whoop, "We won!" We're both breathing hard but happy, and dreams of being a famous jockey like Abe Hawkins swim in my head.

Slipping off Aristo's back, I bow real low to the willow tree. "I, Gabriel Alexander, winning jockey, want to thank all you fine ladies—"

"Gabriel Alexander, that horse must have kicked you in

your head," a sassy voice interrupts me. "You're no winning jockey. You're nothing but a puny stable boy in raggedy britches!"

Startled, I jerk my head up. Annabelle's peering at me through the veil of willow branches. She's wearing a fancy straw hat and a yellow dress with a puffy skirt. A basket of meadow flowers hangs from one arm, and daisies poke from her hat ribbon.

"And you ain't no fine lady!" I shoot back, mad that she caught me bowing to a tree. Annabelle's a slave like me, but she grew up in the Main House. Since Master and Mistress have no children, they spoil her like a daughter.

Annabelle's eyes grow squinty. "If Mistress Jane didn't need these flowers to cheer her, I'd dump them over your braggety head." Spreading the branches like curtains, she sashays toward the kitchen garden.

"Least then I'd smell sweeter than you!" I holler.

"Least *I* can read and write!" she tosses over her shoulder. Annabelle always wants the last word.

I clench my fists. Since she gets schooling from Mistress Jane, Annabelle loves to throw her learning in my face. But today it don't bother me for long, 'cause I've got a bigger boast. "Least *I'm* riding to the big city of Lexington where you ain't *never* been! You don't do nothing but stay home tending the sick."

"Humph." Annabelle slams shut the gate into the garden. "You only going 'cause you the skinniest stable boy. Not 'cause you some fine rider like *Mister* Jackson."

Her mocking burns me up. Old Uncle, the yard slave, is

in the kitchen garden picking peas. I see his body twitch with laughter. I loosen my tongue, determined not to let Annabelle get the last taunt.

"Sass me all you want, Miss Annabelle. But one day you'll use your fine learning to read about *me* in the *Lexington Observer*! And the words will say, 'Gabriel Alexander, Winning Jockey!'"

Sticking her nose in the air, Annabelle struts up the brick path to the summer kitchen, pretending she don't care. Only I know she cares 'cause she's switching her hind end back and forth like an angry horse. Too bad I ain't got time to gloat. Renny, the coachman, is driving the wagon and team into the stable yard, and I see Master Giles striding down the front walk from the Main House. I best hurry and get Tenpenny ready before Pa starts bellowing for me.

I race to the barn, bare feet pounding the dry grass. Tenpenny's head is hanging over the stall door. His eyes are keen. Grabbing the bridle off the hook, I open the door. He ducks into the corner, not wanting the metal bit in his mouth. I talk sweet until he comes around. Then I stand on a wooden bucket and slip the bit into his mouth and the headstall over his ears.

Clucking, I run the colt outside. Master Giles sits in the wagon on the seat next to Renny. Jackson's slouched on a pile of sacks in the wagon bed. Pa's helping two stable hands load the last of the feed, tack, and supplies. Cook Nancy passes Jackson a basket of vittles. I lick my lips, hoping she's packed some of her homemade bread.

Master nods approvingly when Tenpenny prances toward

the wagon. "Horse looks fine," he tells Pa, who hoists me up onto the colt's bare back.

Three mounted men are heading down the lane. I recognize Mister Ham and his two grown sons, Beale and Henry, farmers from down the pike. Master hires them when he needs an armed escort. All three men tote double holsters on their saddle pommels. A shotgun lies across Master Giles's lap and a pistol peeks from under his topcoat.

"Morning, Winston." Mister Ham halts his gelding, a big-boned Kentucky Saddler.

"Morning, Ham." Master Giles nods. "Glad you brought your sons. Reports from Georgetown aren't good. Yesterday, One Arm and his Rebel raiders robbed the citizens and burned the telegraph office. Union soldiers chased them out of town but lost them in the hollows. I've left armed guards here at the farm in case they ride this far."

I catch my breath. Georgetown is north of Lexington. That means One Arm Dan Parmer and his band of Confederate raiders might run into us on the road. God willing, they won't venture to Lexington since Union troops are camped there.

Pa told me that most of Kentucky is Union, which means a lot of folks here are rooting for the Yankees from the North. But the Confederates have plenty of friends in Kentucky, too. Seems every valley holds farmers and shopkeepers who are Rebels at heart. They aid One Arm and his men every chance they get. Some say the raiders are out to win the war for the South. I say they're robbers bent on stealing what they want from either side. And what they want most is *horses*, especially swift Thoroughbreds like Tenpenny.

I glance at Pa. His expression is grave as he climbs into the wagon bed beside Jackson. Everyone at Woodville Farm has heard stories about One Arm and his band of raiders: How they'll ride into a farm and steal it blind. How they'll kick a colored man bloody. How they'll swipe a horse right out from under its rider then gallop it to death.

At the thought of meeting One Arm and his men, a shiver sweeps through my bones. Tenpenny dances beneath me, eager to go. Only now I ain't so sure about this journey. I lay my hand against the colt's warm neck, and my excitement turns to fear.

CHAPTER TWO

Renny slaps the reins, the wagon jolts forward, and we head down the lane that curves in front of the Main House. Annabelle stands on the wide marble steps.

"Don't fall off, *boy*," she calls to me with false sweetness.

On the porch, Mistress Jane waves goodbye from her wheelchair. Her face is so pale, it disappears against the white of her shawl. Ma stands beside the wheelchair, a patterned headscarf wrapped around her hair. Usually she wears it proud, like a queen's crown, but this morning, the folds sag. A handkerchief is pressed against her mouth, and I see tears in her eyes.

"Don't worry about me, Ma," I call, straightening my spine so she—and Annabelle—can see I'm *not* a boy. I'm as tall and brave as a man and ready for this journey. But Ma's gaze isn't on me. Weeping, she runs down the steps toward the wagon. Pa hops out, she falls in his arms, and for a second they hold each other.

I'm so surprised, I halt Tenpenny. When Pa climbs back into the moving wagon, Ma covers her face with her hands.

Sobbing mightily, she races up the steps and into the Main House. Ma's used to Pa's leaving for races in other towns, so I ain't sure why she's so weepy. And when I give Annabelle a questioning look, I see her expression is as startled as mine.

Then Tenpenny leaps after the wagon, not wanting to be left behind. As our band clip-clops down the lane, there's no holding back the colt. He prances ahead, mouthing his bit. When we turn east on Frankfort Pike, Henry and Beale ride to my right and left. The wagon follows behind us. Beyond the dust of the wagon wheels, Mister Ham brings up the rear.

As we trot along, I forget the odd scene between Ma and Pa back at the farm. I even forget One Arm and his raiders. Tenpenny's so full of oats, he takes all my attention. When we cross Elkhorn Creek, the echo of his hooves on the bridge sends him bolting. Just when I get him settled, he startles at the squirrels in the overhanging branches. A half-mile later, he shies at the cows slapping flies with their tails beside the stone fence, and when a chipmunk skitters across the road, he rears in terror.

The whole time, Beale and Henry are chuckling.

"Henry, you think we should bet on that horse tomorrow?" Beale asks his brother. "Looks like he's scared of his own shadow."

Henry shakes his head. "Naw. Better we put our money on that Thoroughbred from the North. What's his name? Jersey Gent?"

"Jersey Gent?" I snort. "He won't beat Penny. You two best lay your money on Tenpenny. He's faster than any horse in Kentucky. 'Cept for Aristo."

"The way I hear it, Aristo's too wild to ride," Henry says.

"I can handle him," I boast. "I can jockey that colt to a win." I crouch on Tenpenny's neck, and he breaks into a canter.

"Gabriel!" Master Giles calls. "Keep that horse fresh."

"Yes sir." Sitting back, I slow the colt to a walk. Pa says it's a long trip to Lexington, and if Tenpenny's to win tomorrow, he'll need his spunk.

Beyond Master's land, we pass a cluster of shanties, and several boys run out to greet us. Their feet are bare, their clothes torn.

"Where you goin'?" they call to me.

"Going to Lexington," I reply. "To race this fine horse."

Their eyes pop with envy. "To town? To race?" They trot alongside Tenpenny, shouting questions up at me, "*You* ridin' him? Who he racin'? He gonna win?"

Arching his neck, Tenpenny sidles away from their clamoring. I tip my chin high. "We aim to win. Wish us luck."

On the other side of me, Beale reaches in his shirt pocket and draws out a handful of pennies. "Go on now, boys, before you get trampled." He tosses the coins in the grass beside the road. They dive for them. I watch them search through the grass, wishing I had a pocketful of pennies to spend in Lexington. But Pa saves every bit of his scant wage. "So one day, I can buy your freedom," he tells Ma and me.

We're nearing an intersection. The sound of hooves pounding on hard dirt signals riders galloping toward us from the north. Beale jerks his head, gesturing for me to fall back. I steer Tenpenny beside the wagon. Jackson's suddenly wide-awake and Pa sits upright. The shotgun is still in Master Giles's lap, but the barrel's aimed toward the oncoming riders.

"That road leads to Georgetown," I hear Pa say in a low voice. I swallow hard. One Arm and his raiders were last spotted in Georgetown.

Mister Ham joins Beale and Henry, and the three halt their horses in the intersection, facing the approaching riders. Their pistols are drawn.

"Howdy!" someone hollers as the group slows their horses in a flurry of dust. "No call for firearms. We're from Locust Run, southwest of Georgetown."

There are four riders, and I see by their homespun shirts and floppy hats that they're farmers riding heavy-legged carriage and plow horses, not raiders riding stolen Thoroughbreds.

"Crenshaw? Is that you?" Mister Ham asks the speaker.

"Yes sir, Mister Ham. It's me, my hired hand, and the Tylers of River Run."

"Why are you men off your land?" Mister Ham asks. "Your horses should be turning soil, not galloping hard roads. Is there more trouble?"

Taking off his hat, Mister Crenshaw wipes his sweaty face with a handkerchief. "You could say. Soldiers chased One Arm and his bunch out of Georgetown, so now they're raiding our farms for supplies and stock. We're riding to Lexington to ask the Union soldiers for help."

"God speed, then. We'll be right behind you."

The farmers bid us good day, then turn their mounts east

toward Lexington. Renny snaps the whip over the wagon horses, and we start off in the same direction. Pa sinks back in the wagon bed, Jackson pulls his hat brim over his eyes, and Master takes his hand off his shotgun.

Only I can't relax. I keep watching for raiders and Union soldiers. I've never seen a Union soldier. Pa says they look right smart in their uniforms. Oh, what I wouldn't give to see a column of Yankees marching toward us right now! Marching for freedom for us slaves.

Mister Ham rides back to the wagon. "We best keep vigilant," he tells Master. "The soldiers in Georgetown may be chasing One Arm this way."

Master Giles nods. "Good. When Crenshaw alerts the troops in Lexington, they should set out this way, too. The soldiers can squeeze those raiders from both directions. It's time those Rebel thieves are caught and hung."

Mister Ham grins in agreement. Beale waves at me to ride up with him and Henry. As we trot along, I think about Master Giles and his allegiance. Master is from England, a place far from Kentucky, and Pa says he straddles the fence where the war is concerned. Master owns land in both England *and* Kentucky. He loves life on Woodville Farm, and doesn't want the Yankees coming here and telling him how to live. Like most other members of the English aristocracy, he leans toward the Southern cause. But at the same time, he doesn't want to get on the bad side of the Northern troops. As a compromise, Master flies the Union Jack, the British flag, over the farm, hoping to stay on good terms with both armies. But lately, since the Confederate Rebels started raiding nearby farms and towns, he's gotten mighty riled up at them. Pa says he wouldn't be surprised if Master's ready to side with the North.

As we near Lexington and there's still no sign of One Arm, I begin to relax. The edge is off Tenpenny, and he's as calm as a cart pony. Letting the reins hang slack, I goggle at the sights. We pass a schoolyard filled with white children jumping rope and shooting marbles. I stare hungrily as the colorful marbles flash in the sunlight. Jase, Tandy, and me make marbles out of clay. Oh, what I wouldn't give for a pouch of sparkly glass ones!

The school falls behind, and Frankfort Pike winds into a ravine where the tall trees hide the sun. The roadside's thick with underbrush. We're halfway to the bottom of the ravine when Tenpenny flattens his ears. Soon I hear what my horse has sensed: the faint thud of pursuing hooves.

Before I can see if it's friend or foe, Master Giles calls out sharply, "Gabriel, hide Tenpenny in the woods. *Now!*"

I obey rabbit-quick, but Tenpenny balks, not wanting to leave the other horses. I pummel him with my bare heels. Finally he bounds through the brush. Briars snag my ankles and branches slap my cheeks as we crash through the woods. The sides of the ravine are craggy and steep, and Tenpenny scrambles for footing. I steer him to a level outcropping. Over my ragged breathing, I hear the jangle of bits and spurs. Through the trees, I glimpse riders spilling over the hill.

"Halt!" someone orders, and the flow of riders stops. Peering between Tenpenny's ears, I see a ragtag assortment of slouch hats, forage caps, and flat-crowned derbies. Dust colors them all Confederate gray.

My skin grows cold. *It's One Arm and his raiders!*

Three riders trot down the pike toward the wagon, which has halted at the bottom of the ravine. Mister Ham, Henry, and Beale ride up to meet them. The six men square off and warily greet each other.

I'm close enough that I can hear them. That means they're close enough to spot *me* if they look. "Shhh," I whisper to Tenpenny, fearful that he'll neigh.

I rise up on the colt's neck, trying to get a better view. If one of the men is One Arm Dan Parmer, I'll know right away. His lower right arm is missing, and folks say he always holds his rifle in the crook of his elbow.

"We're heading into Lexington for supplies," Mister Ham tells the Rebels. "We have nothing of value."

"I'll be the judge of that," the rider in the middle replies. He wears an officer-style slouch hat and military jacket. His horse steps forward, toward the wagon, but Mister Ham and his sons don't budge.

"Move out of my way," the man orders, "or I'll give the word, and my men will gladly ransack the wagon." When he turns in his saddle, I spy the empty shirtsleeve tied up below his elbow. It's got to be One Arm!

Beale levels his pistol barrel at the man's face. "Give the word and *you'll* be dead."

Just then Master Giles walks up from the bottom of the ravine. "I say, gents," he calls out, exaggerating his British accent. He carries the shotgun loosely as if the sight of a band of armed riders is no threat. "No cause for hard words. We are all on the same side. Captain Parmer, I presume?" He directs his question to the man in the middle, though I've never heard anyone say that One Arm's a real captain.

The slouch hat bobs. "And you are Mister Winston Giles of Woodville Farm?"

"I am, sir. There's no reason to take my men and wagon by force. Mister Ham is telling the truth. We are on our way to Lexington to procure supplies. Except for my colored men, my wagon is empty."

One Arm seems to consider this. Or maybe he's considering the pistol pointed at his face.

Master Giles raises one hand. "However, I do believe I can spare some cash for the Confederate cause. Enough to buy you and your men supplies in Versailles? I presume you'll be headed in that direction since I have word that Union soldiers from Lexington are riding after you, perhaps headed this way as we speak."

One Arm shifts in his saddle. A sly grin crinkles his sunbrowned cheeks. "Then I'll accept your offer, Mister Giles. I like a man who knows the value of cash and the worth of helpful information."

Master Giles digs in his trouser pocket and draws out a leather pouch. My eyes widen. Not only is he warning One Arm about the Union soldiers, he's paying off the robbers! I was wrong. Master's a Confederate through and through.

Reaching down, One Arm opens his gloved left hand, and Master drops several gold coins in his palm. When the captain straightens, he pockets the money and then tips his hat. "Much obliged for the gold and information, Mister Giles. And I hope we meet again when the South is victorious. Come on, boys," One Arm calls, reining his horse around. Suddenly, he jerks back on the rein and stares in my direction.

I duck down on Tenpenny's neck, but it's too late. He's seen us. No matter how brave Beale and Henry are, we're sorely outnumbered. If One Arm gives the word, his men will kill us all. Then they'll steal Tenpenny and, with whip and spurs, ride him to his death.

"What're you trying to pull, Giles?" Taking out his pistol, One Arm cocks it with his good hand. The barrel points right at my face. "You've got a horse hidden in those woods, which means it's more valuable than your gold coins. Tell your men to stand aside, 'cause *I* aim to fetch it!"

CHAPTER THREE

"D ear Jesus," I mumble into the colt's mane, "don't let
One Arm shoot me and steal my horse." I press my
cheek into Tenpenny's sweaty neck, afraid to
breathe.

"Captain Parmer, if I were you, I wouldn't waste my
time," Master Giles says, his voice polite, but hard, too. "It's
just my lookout. Any delay might cause your capture—or
your death."

The air is filled with silence. Feeling my fear, Tenpenny
paws nervously. *Do something,* I tell myself. If I can get the
colt to open ground, there ain't no Rebel can catch us.

I peer around the woods, hunting for an escape route. To
my right, the hill rises steeply. To my left, it drops into a
ravine. I'm looking behind me when I hear the clank of
spurs and the creak of leather. Dare I believe my ears?
Cautiously I peek toward the road. Sweet Jesus has answered
my prayers. The raiders are leaving!

One Arm holsters his pistol. "If you are lying to me,
you'll regret your bravado, Mister Giles," he declares. Wheel-
ing his horse, he gallops up the pike after his men.

I collapse like an empty saddlebag. The sound of rustling and crackling makes me look up. Pa's fighting his way through the brush.

"Gabriel?" he calls worriedly. "You all right?"

"I'm fine, Pa." I bite my lip to keep it from quivering. When Pa reaches us, he drags me off the colt and wraps me safe in his arms. For a second, I let his strength calm me. Then I pull away. "I'm *mighty* fine now those Rebels are gone. Penny and me were fixing to run if they came after us."

Pa's face shines with relief. "And where were you planning on running to? You and Penny ain't deer."

"Oh, me and Penny could outrace those raiders," I boast. "No Confederate's going to get my horse."

Pa fixes me with a stern gaze. "Tenpenny ain't your horse, Gabriel. Besides, no horse is worth a man's life."

I drop my gaze to my bare feet. I don't want to argue with Pa, but only a coward would save himself and leave his horse for those thieves.

"Isaac! Gabriel!" Master Giles hollers from the road. "We better get a move on before Captain Parmer changes his mind."

Pa boosts me back on to Tenpenny and leads us out of the woods. Master's boarding the wagon. Mister Ham and his sons are watching the crest of the hill as if expecting more unwanted company.

We set off at a good clip, and when we trot from that dark ravine, I breathe easier. Soon the houses and farms grow closer together, and we ride into Lexington. I thought nothing could be as exciting as meeting One Arm, but I'm mistaken. The city is a wonder.

Mouth flapping, eyes popping, I ride down a wide street made of stones. Churches, hotels, and shops—not trees and scrub—line both sides. The buildings stand wall to wall with rows of windows glinting in the daylight. Chimneys and spires jut from sloped roofs, and signs arch over every door. If Annabelle were here, she'd be reading up a storm!

Since I can't read, I 'cipher the shopkeepers' wares by noting the goods hanging from awnings and displayed in windows: loaves of bread and shiny leather boots and fancy ladies' hats. As I move down the street, I spot other items for sale: guitars, cigars, even fish that look freshly caught and strung up.

Why, a person can buy just about anything in Lexington!

Tenpenny's jumping at all the sights, but Beale's and Henry's horses are used to the commotion. They ride close, keeping the colt from bolting.

"Mister Beale, what's that say?" I ask, pointing to a building ahead. Swirly letters have been painted on the side of the store right on the brick!

"It says Curtis Confectionery."

"Con…fec…sh-shun," I stammer, giving up when the word ties my tongue.

Beale chuckles. "That means the shop sells sweets."

"Mmm." My mouth begins to water, and I remember I haven't eaten since morning mush.

Turning to his father, Beale says, "The danger is over, sir, and the horse seems calm. Permission for Henry and me to catch up with you later at the hotel."

"Permission granted," Mister Ham tells his sons.

I watch longingly as they rein their mounts toward the stores. We've been riding all day, and I'm eager to stretch my legs and get a closer look at that sweet shop. At the thought of a licorice twist, my stomach growls. But no luck. Everyone else keeps moving along the street at a slow pace.

Tenpenny falls back beside the wagon bed. Pa tosses me a roasted sweet potato from the basket by his feet and gives Jackson a slice of Cook Nancy's homemade bread.

As I bite into my potato, I stare at the sights. Lexington's busy with more folks than I've seen in my life. They're strolling along the walks and clustered around doorways. Half the faces are as black as mine, and Jackson tips his hat to all the colored ladies.

"Morning, Miss Pearl," he calls. "Good day, Miss Adele."

"I believe Mr. Jackson knows every lady in Lexington," I say to Pa.

Finally Renny stops the wagon in front of a three-story hotel. Carriages wait out front, the coachmen holding the reins of the horses. On the pillared porch, gentlemen in top hats smoke and talk.

I eye the hotel. One day, when I'm famous like Abe Hawkins, I'll stay in a fancy hotel, too. For now, though, I've got to bunk at the racetrack with Pa, Jackson, and Renny.

Master gives Mister Ham and Pa instructions and then

bids us good day. Renny carries Master's valise to the porch, handing it over to a servant. Then we head off.

Delivery wagons and carriages rattle past as we continue out of town. The sun is high, and Tenpenny's neck is dark with sweat.

When we reach the racetrack, Mister Ham escorts us past the wooden grandstand to a long, low barn. I can't see the track, but Jackson tells me it's a mile long with the finish line in front of the grandstand. "So all the ladies can throw kisses at me when I win," he says with a chuckle.

We stop at the far end of the barn in front of two empty stalls bedded with straw. Pa climbs from the wagon, his legs stiff. Jackson jumps nimbly out and strides off to join a group of colored men jawing by a fire in a cleared area beneath a grove of trees. Other jockeys, I gather. Seeing them laughing and talking has me wishing *I* was a jockey.

Tired, I slip off Tenpenny and lead him into the stall. He neighs loudly. Several horses answer. I unbridle the colt and give him a few sips of water, then leave him to munch a flake of hay while I help Pa and Renny unload the wagon. Soon the second stall is filled with two ticking-covered pallets, blankets, bundles of hay, and a sack of feed. When the wagon's empty, Renny takes the team down to the livery. Mister Ham's already gone back to town, so it's just Pa and me.

"Unwrap Penny's legs," Pa says. "I'll fetch a bucket of water from the pump so you can wash him down."

"Yes sir." I take a halter in to Tenpenny. He butts me, then tries to scratch his nose on my shoulder. I push his head away, showing him who's boss. For the rest of the afternoon,

I wash, walk, and groom Tenpenny. While I work, I keep my ears pricked for news. Pa and Jackson spend much of their time chatting with the other trainers and jockeys. I find out there are three races tomorrow. Tenpenny's in the second one, racing against five other horses. By sundown, Pa and Jackson have eyeballed every one of the entries. Now they're sitting on wooden boxes outside the stall door, and while I bed Tenpenny down for the night, I catch snatches of their discussion of tomorrow's race.

"The Louisville horse, Famous Tom, will be carrying weight," Jackson says, keeping his voice low, "'cause his jockey's light."

"Looks like Jersey Gent, the horse from up North, had a spavin the last race," Pa adds, sipping coffee from a tin cup. "I noticed the swelling on his hock. And Judge Fahill's entered his nag, Virgil."

Jackson whistles. "That broken-down colt? He should be put out to pasture."

"The Judge probably wants to run up the bets on the other horses. What do you hear about Doctor Rammer's mare, Lilith, from Lexington? Who's jockeying her?"

Jackson snorts. "Rammer's slave Levi is riding. He'll fall off when that mare leaps at the starting drum. And I hear word that the jockey from Louisville spurs his mount over the finish line."

Spurs! I snort, echoing Jackson. One thing I know for sure: a horse needs a gentle hand.

"Sounds like the entry to watch is Blue Belle," Pa says.

Jackson nods in agreement. "She's a fine mare, and Mister

Parris brought a slave from Virginia to ride her."

"They'll never beat you and Penny," I say from the stall.

"You're right there." Standing, Jackson adjusts his shirt cuffs and vest. "Enough talk. It's high time I get to town." He winks at me before he strides off. "Before the lovely ladies start to miss me."

Minutes later, Pa comes in the stall and runs his hand down Tenpenny's legs, checking for heat or puffiness. Then we picnic by the fire with the other grooms and trainers, trading a loaf of Cook Nancy's bread for coffee and bacon. By the time we finish eating, my jaws are cracking with yawns. Pa throws me a blanket before bedding down in the spare stall. I'm tuckered out, but I want to check the track before I curl up with Tenpenny. I haven't had a chance to see it since we rode up.

I listen for Pa's snoring and then jog past the campfire. A few blanket-wrapped bodies lie on the ground around it, and two men sit on a log drinking from tin cups. Past the fire, it's darker.

Slowly, I make my way toward the wooden grandstand. A white fence surrounds the wide dirt track. Leaning on the top rail, I stare down the track to the first bend. It's too dark to see much farther, but I can pretend I'm a jockey, galloping my horse to the finish line, the folks in the grandstand hallooing.

I'm picturing it so clearly, I really hear the halloos.

The chorus grows louder and I realize it's singing. Voices as haunting as whippoorwills are coming from the other side of the track.

Who's singing at this late hour? I wonder. Ducking under the rail, I climb the steps into the grandstand until I can see across the track. There's a line of trees on the other side of the far railing. Beyond the trees, I spot dozens of fires lighting the hillside like stars in the sky. Men in blue uniforms stand around the fires, and I catch my breath: *Yankees!*

I patter down the grandstand steps and vault over the rail onto the dirt track. I can't leave Lexington without seeing a real soldier.

I trot around the track to the other side, my bare feet sinking in the soft dirt. Then I climb over the far fence rail, jump to the ground, and wind through the grass to the border of trees. Hiding behind a thick trunk, I stare at the hillside. Rows of white tents stripe the sloping field, and stacked rifles poke skyward.

A circle of soldiers, two deep, is standing around a fire, singing. I'm close enough to see the sparkle of uniform buttons and the gleam of white teeth in black faces.

It's a company of *colored* soldiers! I'm so surprised I almost fall over. The chorus dies down, and one man's voice booms out, deep and rich, "*I walk in de battlefield, I'll walk through de battlefield.*"

The others join in: "*I'll walk in de battlefield, I'll walk through de battlefield. To lay dis body down. To fight for de freedom land.*"

My heart soars with their voices. Pa's talked about colored men, both slave and free, who have joined the Union army. Oh, how I wish I could be a soldier and fight for freedom, too.

The snap of a twig makes me start. Then someone grabs my shirt collar and yanks me backward. "Let go!" I yell. Kicking and twisting, I try to get away.

"Hold still, boy," a deep voice commands. I glimpse the blue sleeve of a soldier's uniform. The hand tightens on the neck of my shirt, and the soldier drags me toward the fire-light. "Lookee what I found!" he hollers to the circle of men.

Abruptly, the singing stops and all eyes turn to me. Letting go, the soldier shoves me, and I stumble toward the fire, too scared to yelp again.

The lone singer steps forward, fists planted on his hips. He's as tall as a tree and has stripes on his coat sleeve.

"Well, well," he thunders so loud my knees knock. "Looks like Private Campbell has found hisself a Confederate spy!"

CHAPTER FOUR

Confederate spy? Fear dries the spit in my mouth, and I stammer so bad that I can't set him straight.

"A *scrawny* spy at that," the soldier booms.

"Must be why he slipped past the guards," Private Campbell says. He squeezes my shoulder like he's feeling a plucked chicken. "Think he's too scrawny to string up, Corporal Blue?"

String up? Thoughts of hanging till I'm dead loosen my tongue and I blurt, "Sir, I ain't no spy!"

"No spy?" Corporal Blue rears back as if astonished. "Then why you hiding in the trees?"

I wave toward the racetrack. "I was yonder and heard your singing, and I wanted to see a Union soldier 'fore I left Lexington. That's all. Oh, please, Corporal *sir*, don't string me up. I jest a slave boy riding horses for Master Giles."

I clasp my fingers together, pleading. His lips are twitching in a smile, and the circle of soldiers bursts into guffaws.

"Boy, we know you ain't no Rebel spy," Corporal Blue

says, not unkindly. "You too clean and well-fed."

"You ain't going to hang me?"

The corporal claps my shoulder. "We just joshing you. Come on, join us by the fire. I'm Corporal Benjamin Blue. What's your name?"

Hesitating, I glance over my shoulder, wondering if Pa's missing me. My fear's slowly dying, but my cheeks grow hot with embarrassment. I pleaded for mercy like a pigeon-hearted Rebel!

Throwing back my shoulders, I muster a speck of dignity. "My name's Gabriel Alexander."

Corporal Blue holds out his hand. "Welcome, Gabriel Alexander, to Company H of the 100th United States Colored Infantry."

I shake his hand, my fingers disappearing in his grip.

"So why you here?" he asks. "A runaway?"

"No sir. I'm from Woodville Farm. My master's got a fine colt entered in the second race tomorrow at the Kentucky Association track."

"Hear that?" Private Campbell calls around. "This boy says there's a fine colt entered in the second race. You figure he going to win?" he addresses me.

I nod firmly. "Tenpenny's the fastest colt in Lexington, and Jackson's the finest jockey."

Suddenly, the men around the campfire erupt. They call out horses' names and lay bets. Tobacco plugs, coins, buckles, pocket watches, and smoking pipes are tossed into a pile. Private Campbell whips out a pencil and starts jotting down bets on the inside cover of a Bible. Seems the men of

Company H have been studying on tomorrow's race!

Corporal Blue watches with an amused expression. "We do more betting than shooting, that's for sure."

"What about fighting?" I ask. Now that there's no threat of hanging, I aim to find out more about Company H.

"Fighting?" Corporal Blue grunts. "We just mustered in. We're so new our boots squeak. 'Sides, we're too busy toting and cooking for the white soldiers to fight Rebels."

"Why are you toting and cooking for whites? You're a Yankee soldier. Ain't you free?"

"Oh, we're free all right. Free to dig latrines, collect firewood, and haul water. Instead of the rifle, we wield the spade and ax. Most of these boys are ex-slaves who don't know nothing 'cept work." Corporal Blue touches the stripes on his shoulder. "Don't misjudge us, though. We're learning to clean our guns and drill, shoot straight, and march double-quick. We're eager to fight. And when we get to Tennessee, we will," he adds with pride.

"And one day I'll join you," I declare. "Then I'll be free, too. And able to fight those Rebels." I make a pretend jab like I've got a bayonet.

He chuckles. "You as skinny as a sapling. Too skinny to march far with a rifle, I reckon. But tag along with us. We can use a smart boy. We'll make you our drummer. Then your new master will be the U.S. Army."

The idea tempts me though I've never tapped a drum. "Company H got any horses?"

"Naw. Only officers and cavalry got horses."

"Then I'll pass." I don't want to tell him how much I'd

miss Ma and Pa, Tenpenny and Aristo. "Maybe after I grow into a man strong as you, I'll join up to fight for freedom."

Corporal Blue laughs. "I believe you will." Then his face turns grave in the firelight. "'Cause freedom, why, that's worth fighting for, Gabriel Alexander. We may be digging latrines today, but one day, we'll be battling those Rebels. Now stay a spell." He steers me toward the fire. "We wants to hear more about tomorrow's race!"

★★★

The next morning, Pa and me are awake before the sun. We feed Tenpenny half-rations, wrap his legs, and rub him glossy. Mornings like this, Pa and me work silent, but companionable. We don't need to talk. We know each other's minds as well as we know horses.

Part of me wants to tell Pa about meeting Corporal Blue and the colored soldiers last night, but another part says, "never mind" 'cause we need to concentrate on winning this race.

When I fetch the bridle from the spare stall, I see Jackson sprawled on the pallet, his mouth wide in a snore. The ladies must have kept him late.

I bridle Tenpenny and lead him from the stall. Pa hands me a cold hoecake. "Walk Penny around the entire track," he says as he throws me up on the colt. "Let him stretch his legs and look at every rock and tree. I don't want him spooking in the middle of the race."

Pa has magic ways with horses, and his ways usually win

31

races, so I don't question him. Chewing my hoecake, I rein Tenpenny toward the track.

The colt wants to play. He bucks in place, rattling my bones.

"Penny, you got four miles of race this noon. You best save your fire," I scold as we jog through a break in the fence. Fog shrouds the grandstand and far side of the track. I aim Tenpenny to the right, and he prances around the bend, his muscles rippling under my legs. Joy fills me. How I long to hear the sound of the starting drum. How I long to race!

When we pass the line of trees bordering the Union camp, I steer Tenpenny to the outside rail. The rising sun illuminates the hillside, and I see soldiers shaking blankets and making coffee. Several lean over basins set on a plank table. Steam rises from the basins, and the soldiers splash water on their faces and lather up to shave.

I hear Corporal Blue's words, "'cause freedom worth fighting for," and for a moment, I pine for camp life.

Tenpenny snorts at a mockingbird. He careens sideways, almost dumping me in the dirt. I squeeze my legs into his side, pushing him forward. The mile track flows and winds like a river. It's smooth in the middle, but banked and crusted along the inside rail. Rocks have been kicked up along the outside rail.

By the time we've walked around the track, the sun is up and the grounds are stirring with folks. Tenpenny's loose, relaxed and hungry. With every step, he tries to snatch a bite of grass or leaves. Jackson's sitting by the fire, head cradled in his hands.

"Did you find some pretty ladies last night, Mister Jackson?" I tease.

Opening one eye, he glares at me.

Pa's in front of the stall with a bucket of molasses, corn, and oats. He pulls off Tenpenny's bridle, and the colt attacks the bucket, tossing grain everywhere.

"Easy, hoss," Pa says as he wraps a rope around Tenpenny's neck. "Don't want you getting colic."

I slide off the colt's back. "Jackson needs to keep to the middle of the track," I tell Pa. "Against either rail be hard on a horse's legs."

Pa nods. "How'd he feel?"

"Right smart." I scratch under Tenpenny's mane. He's happily slobbering grain. I figure the colt doesn't know what he's in for. The race for three- and four-year-olds is two heats of two miles each. By the last mile, he'll be leg sore and heart weary.

"Pick out his stall, Gabriel," Pa says. "Then fetch two buckets of water. I want one simmering on the fire. I'm taking him down to the creek."

"Yes sir." I hurry to the stall with basket and pitchfork. All across the grounds, horses whinny and men cuss. Several folks come by Tenpenny's stall asking for the colt. This is Tenpenny's first race, and all the trainers and owners want to get a good look at Woodville Farm's latest entry.

I don't tell them where Tenpenny is. I know that Pa has taken Tenpenny down to the creek not only to let the cold water firm the colt's legs, but also to keep him away from the crowd. Pa doesn't want some greedy owner poisoning

Tenpenny's bucket of water or pricking him in the hock with a needle—sure ways to keep a horse from winning.

The sun's overhead when Master Giles stops by. I've finished cleaning the stall and fetching water, and I'm sitting on a bucket, wiping down Tenpenny's bridle so it's soft and supple.

"Morning, Gabriel." He's dressed like a gentleman in derby and frock coat, and he's carrying an ivory-handled cane.

I drop the bridle and jump to my feet. "Morning, sir."

"How's the colt?"

"Rip-roaring, but he listened to my legs and hands. Jackson will be able to ride him to victory."

Master points at me with his cane. "You've got the mind of a horseman like your pa, Gabriel."

"Thank you, sir."

"Get on with your work now." He heads into the crowd. By now, the grounds are filling with gentlefolk: men sporting top hats and ladies wearing hoop skirts. They climb into the grandstands. Their slaves wait by the carriages with picnic baskets, lawn chairs, and blankets. Working folks, black and white, crowd the rails, and everyone carries on like it's a party. Seems like Lexington doesn't know there's a war going on.

I miss all of the first race 'cause I'm too busy walking Tenpenny, who's wound as tight as Pa's pocket watch. The colt throws his head, bumps me with his nose, and drags me hither and yon. I don't scold 'cause I know he's just scared.

I lead him toward the grandstand, which erupts with

cheering, and I gather the first race is over. Minutes later, a gray mare limps from the track, her head hanging. A roan walks behind her, shaking with fatigue. The winner stands in the middle of the track. His heaving sides are dotted with spur marks, and his flared nostrils are red rimmed. His colored jockey tries to smile, but his lips are cracked and swollen. The owner stands beside them, fat-bellied and smug as he accepts the trophy and $1,500 purse. Some of the crowd cheers, while others boo. Along the rail, money exchanges hands, and several men get in fistfights.

My heart tightens. I stroke Tenpenny's neck, hoping he'll reach the finish line with ears and head high. We've conditioned the colt for weeks, and Pa doesn't believe in spurs or whips, but hard running takes its toll on any horse.

Pa comes over, carrying the saddle and sheepskin pad he's made special so Tenpenny's back doesn't get sore. Jackson strides beside him looking smart in his silks. He wears black boots, doeskin breeches, and a blue shirt and gold cap, Woodville's colors.

I lead the colt into the circle of onlookers, joining the five other entries. Master Giles watches with the owners. They're talking among themselves, downplaying their horse's abilities, hoping to raise the betting odds.

Pa says a man could win a year's wages if he placed the right bet. I sigh, wishing Pa was a betting man. Then I could buy a hoop skirt for Ma, and Pa could buy our freedom.

The bugle announces the parade to the track. Pa gives Jackson a leg up into the saddle. Jackson rides with short stirrups so he can stay off the horse's back. Most other jockeys ride English style: They sit straight up with longer stirrups. Pa checks the girth one last time, murmurs last-minute instructions, and then stands back.

"Run like the wind, Penny," I whisper before letting go of the rein. As the horses enter the track, Pa and me push our way to the rail to eye each entry. Pa points out things, and I tuck them in my mind for when I'm training my own horses.

"Girth is too slack on Famous Tom." He nods toward a rangy gray. "Halfway through the first heat of the race, the colt will sweat off weight, and the saddle's going to slip."

Next comes the horse from the north. "Jersey Gent's got that spavin, so he's favoring his right hind leg. If Jackson crowds him to the outside rail, the colt will break down."

When a shiny sorrel jogs past, Pa shakes his head. "Doctor Rammer's mare Lilith is nice, but the jockey Levi won't make it through the whole race. The stewards had to attach pouches of lead shot to the saddle to make weight. A jockey's got to be light, Gabriel, but he's also got to be tough."

I'm light and tough, I think as I study Levi. He's not much older than me, and slight-built like me, but he acts like a whipped hunting dog. Pa says Doctor Rammer is mean to his slaves, and I count my blessings that Master Giles is good to us.

"How about Virgil?" I ask when a tall bay walks past. The colt's nose is high, and his eyes roll.

Pa frowns. "Judge Fahill doesn't care 'bout his horses. And Virgil, well, he's 'bout run to death."

Last to come past is Blue Belle, a sleek red-bay with four white socks. The Virginia jockey sits proud in the saddle, and Belle dances by like she's the Queen of Lexington.

"That's the one to beat," Pa notes.

By now, my heart's pattering with excitement. Across the track, I see a line of men in blue uniforms crowding against the outside rail. They're waving caps and shouting hoorahs. Seems betting *does* come before drilling.

I nudge Pa. "Look, colored soldiers."

The bugle trumpets, and in front of the grandstand, the six horses attempt to line up. Pa explains that the man at the starting line holding the drum is the Jockey Club president. Next to him is a steward, who watches to see when the horses are straight.

Tenpenny's against the inside rail since he's drawn the inside post position. Next to him is Blue Belle, then Jersey Gent, Virgil, and Famous Tom. Lilith is on the outside, and Levi is having problems settling her behind the line. The crowd roars, the mare rears, and Levi almost tumbles off.

Then, for a blink, the horses are lined up even, and the Jockey Club president taps the drum. Tenpenny leaps forward with the others. Jackson reins him sharply to the middle of the track before taking hold and easing the colt to a slow gallop. There are two miles in this first heat, and he doesn't want Tenpenny to give out early.

As the horses make their way down the backstretch, they bunch tight, except for Famous Tom, who takes the lead. "In the first heat, the horse needs to run a mile in a little under two minutes," Pa explains. He's got his watch in his hand to keep time. "Anything faster, he'll burn out. Slower, he won't make the distance."

"What's the distance?"

"See that flag yonder?" He points to a white flag sticking up on the rail about forty feet before the finish line. "When the lead horse crosses the finish line in this first heat, any horses that haven't reached that flag are eliminated. That keeps riders from pulling a Sweeny."

I give Pa a blank look and he explains, "A Sweeny is when a rider holds his horse back in the first heat, trying to save energy for the next heat."

Suddenly, all the horses disappear from sight. "Dangerous spot there," Pa says. "Even the judges can't see. Jockeys could be whipping each other—or worse."

I gnaw my lip, wondering what "worse" could mean. I spot Master Giles high in the grandstand, his field glasses trained on the dip. Behind him are ladies wearing flower-covered hats like they have gardens growing on their heads. The ladies clap excitedly, and I turn to see the horses barreling toward us down the homestretch.

Tenpenny's in the middle. As he canters past, Pa yells for Jackson to keep a hold until the last turn. I watch the colt gallop around the bend. His neck's arched, so I know he ain't weary yet.

Before I know it, they're racing down the homestretch again. This time, the horses are sprawled out. Tenpenny's third in line with Blue Belle right beside him. Both look winded yet strong. Famous Tom crosses first, but just like Pa predicted, the saddle slips and the jockey pitches sideways.

Lilith is second. As they cross the finish line, Levi yanks the reins. But he can't slow the mare, and two grooms dash off after them. Blue Belle comes in third, beating Penny by a nose. Jersey Gent and Virgil canter up last. Virgil's so far behind, he won't make the distance, and Jersey Gent's favoring his right leg. The first heat is over.

"Those two look done for. What in thunder!" Pa says suddenly, and he leaps over the rail onto the track.

Jackson's bent over Tenpenny's withers, clasping his right elbow. He's dropped the reins, and Tenpenny's walking free. "Gabriel," Pa calls over his shoulder as he hurries toward them. "Come quick."

I clamber over the fence and run to grab the colt's dangling reins.

Jackson grimaces as Pa helps him dismount. "Believe my arm's broke."

"How?" Pa asks.

"Famous Tom's jockey had a stick hidden up his sleeve. When we raced into that dip, he whacked at Penny's head. I reached out to keep him from hitting the horse and he got *me* instead."

Even I know what that means. "Pa, that's a foul."

Jackson shakes his head. "Not if the judges didn't see it, Gabriel. That jockey can claim I hit him first."

"What are you going to do?" I loosen Tenpenny's girth and, leading the puffing colt, follow Pa and Jackson from the track.

Pa shrugs. "Ain't no way Jackson can ride with a busted arm, Gabriel."

"But we came all this way to race," I protest. Worried, I glance up at the grandstand. Master Giles is staring down at us with a puzzled frown. Then I look behind me at the Union soldiers, remembering how they bet all their money and goods. "Folks are counting on Penny to win!"

"Then I reckon there's only one thing to do." Using his good arm, Jackson takes off his cap and sets it on my head. "*You* going to have to ride this colt to victory, Gabriel."

CHAPTER FIVE

Mⁱ-m-me?" I stutter. "I ain't never rode a race before!"

"Then it's time," Jackson says. "You ride as good as any boy here."

"*Pa,*" I protest, knowing he'll set Jackson straight. "Tell him I can't—"

But Pa's nodding in agreement with Jackson. "It's settled. You're the colt's jockey for the next heat, Gabriel, but that don't meant you ain't still his groom. We got thirty minutes to get him cooled and ready."

Taking the reins from me, he leads Tenpenny toward the barn. I stand frozen. Horses, riders, and bettors jostle past, but I'm barely aware of them.

Jackson bumps me on the arm. "Ain't any harder than exercising Penny around Mister Giles's field. 'Sides, ain't you the one always crowing about being a winning jockey? This here's your chance." He grimaces in pain. "Now I best find the blacksmith and see if he can do up this arm. You come with me. You'll need my silks." Before I can answer, he strides off, his elbow cocked awkwardly.

I knock myself on the forehead, wondering if I'm dreaming. Sure I want to jockey one day, *but I ain't ready today!*

Forcing my heavy feet to move, I start after Jackson. I find him by the blacksmith's fire. The burly smith is scratching his whiskered chin and studying Jackson's arm. Together, we help Jackson take off his shirt and boots, and I put them on. My bare feet slip around in the boots; my hands almost disappear in the long shirtsleeves.

"They'll have to do," Jackson says. "Now go help your Pa with Penny. My arm's broke, but that don't mean the colt can't win this race."

"But Jackson, how do I ride him? How do I pace him so he ain't too tuckered to win?"

Jackson winces as the blacksmith binds his arm. "Just listen to the horse, Gabriel," he says between clenched teeth. "Listen to Penny. He'll tell you how to set the pace."

I back away, frustrated. That's *no* kind of help. Turning, I run back to the barn. The sleeves of his shirt flap like wings, and I trip over the too-big boots.

Pa's wiping down Tenpenny with the water I had warming on the fire. Master Giles stands near, a concerned expression on his face. When he sees me in the baggy silks, he furrows his brow.

"Isaac, do you have any idea what you're doing?" Master asks Pa.

Pa doesn't even look at him. "You know the boy can ride, sir. You know he's got the gift."

My eyes widen in surprise. I've never heard Pa brag about me before.

"All right then. I'll clear it with the stewards." Master rubs his chin and studies me as if he finds me lacking. Before leaving, he says to Pa, "Just remember, a lot is riding on this race."

"Yes sir, Mister Giles." Pa splashes the last of the water on Penny's legs. "Don't just stand there, Gabriel. Grab a rag and start rubbing."

Silent, we dry off Tenpenny, rewrap his legs, and saddle him. There's so much I want to ask Pa about riding in a race, but my tongue's in a knot. Then I hear the toot of the bugle, and there's no time left for questions.

"I raised the stirrups high, Gabriel," Pa tells me. "Hunch low on Penny's neck. Last heat is the roughest, and I don't want you a target for whips and sticks."

Pa leads Tenpenny to the track. I walk beside him, gaze lowered. I don't *need* to look to know that folks are riled up about the jockey change. Men are already calling out new odds, "Ten dollars to one that Blue Belle will win!" Someone pelts me with a dirt clod. Another calls me an ugly name. A chant rises from the grandstand: "We want Jackson, we want Jackson…"

"Don't listen to them, Gabriel," Pa says. "This race ain't about the crowd. This race is only about you and *your horse.*" Halting Tenpenny, Pa looks me square in the eyes like I'm a man. "Horses always be honest. If you be honest back, they'll give you their hearts."

Gripping my shoulder, he draws me close in a hug. "I

love you, son," he whispers. Then he abruptly straightens, cups my bent knee, and boosts me onto Tenpenny.

My fingers tremble as I gather the reins. Noise from the crowd swirls around my head. I'm drowning in colors and confusion. *I can't do this!* I want to tell Pa.

In front of me, Levi's having problems with Lilith again. He's fighting with the horse, which then bolts onto the track, almost running several folks over. Suddenly, a man carrying a hunting whip ducks under the rail. He cracks Levi across the shoulder and hollers, "Ride that beast and win, you worthless darky!"

I cringe like *I* was struck.

A steward runs the man back into the grandstand. Before I ride through the gap, I kick off Jackson's boots, which plop to the ground. Boos and hisses greet me as Tenpenny jogs onto the track, but I pretend I don't hear.

My bare toes find the stirrups. Pa's right: With them set high, I'm balanced over the saddle pommel. The colt's ears are pricked; his gait's bouncy. I feel the rhythm of his stride, the spring of his legs, the strength of his muscles.

When I press my palm against Tenpenny's warm neck, the hoots of anger seem to disappear, and excitement fills me. *This is what I was born to do.*

Steering Tenpenny against the inside rail, I steal a glance right. There are four other horses lined up for this last heat: Blue Belle, Famous Tom, Jersey Gent, and Lilith. Famous Tom's jockey catches my eye. He makes a whacking motion with his hand.

I snap my head around and face front. "You and me best

steer clear of that boy," I whisper to Tenpenny.

The steward dashes in front of us, checking to see if the horses are even. I lean low and twine my fingers in Tenpenny's mane, pretending I'm at Woodville Farm, bareback on Aristo. When the Jockey Club president taps on his drum, I dig my heels into the colt's sides and shout a soldier's "hoorah." The colt shoots from the line, but I'm clinging burr tight.

We gallop to the front. I tug on the right rein, and Tenpenny swerves to the middle of the track. As we fly down the backstretch, the Yankee soldiers pump their arms and wave their caps. They're a blur when we pass by and head for the dip.

Tenpenny's still in front. I know Pa is yelling, "Don't burn him out!" but I'm pushing to keep ahead of Famous Tom's jockey.

The sound of pounding hooves fills my ears, and Famous Tom pulls aside. I tilt my head. The jockey's brandishing a stick. I tense, expecting the blow to hit me full on, but Tenpenny swings left, and the stick whacks against my shoulder.

As we round the homestretch bend, Famous Tom disappears in our dust. Blue Belle and Lilith are on the inside rail. Jersey Gent is behind on my right, battling it out with Famous Tom. From the corner of my eye I can see both jockeys, whips flailing. They're using them on their horses and on each other.

I slow Tenpenny down the homestretch, hoping to catch sight of Pa. But there's such a roar of noise and a waving of arms, I don't hear or see him, and we fly by in a panic.

There's another mile left, and I don't know how I'm going to make it to the finish, let alone *win* this race!

Then I think back to Jackson's advice. Closing my eyes, I *listen* to Tenpenny.

I hear the steady *whoosh whoosh* of his breathing and the rhythmic drumbeat of his stride. When I squint my eyes open, I see that his ears are pricked and his neck tucked as we canter around the bend for the last mile.

Tenpenny is telling me, *I can run forever, Gabriel.*

Now all *I* got to do is hold on.

The first mile has taken its toll, and I grit my teeth against the pain in my arms, fingers, and legs. My shoulder aches where the stick struck me. Dirt fills my eyes and mouth as Tenpenny gallops down the backstretch. The stirrup irons cut into the bottoms of my bare feet. The muscles in my back cramp, and I tangle one hand in Tenpenny's mane, trying to stay balanced.

Don't give up, I tell myself as we head again into the dip. *You're almost home.*

Then I hear it: the thunder of flying hooves. Blue Belle is sneaking up beside me, and her jockey's grinning 'cause he knows I'm wore out.

Only Tenpenny ain't. He eyes that filly with hate. Pinning his ears, he stretches his neck, yanking the reins through my sore fingers. Side by side, the two horses fly around the last bend toward the finish line. Blue Belle's jockey is pushing his filly with voice and spurs. I'm so tuckered, I can barely hang on. Tenpenny's nostrils are wide and pink, and froth flies from his mouth.

"Go, Penny," I whisper through wind-dried lips.

The colt flicks his ears and, with a surge of power, pulls away from Blue Belle. At that moment I know that he's given me his heart, just like Pa said.

We cross the finish line ahead by a nose.

The crowd explodes. Tenpenny slows to a ragged trot, and I feel myself slipping from the saddle. Pa catches me before I fall.

"You did it, Gabriel," he says proudly.

"No, Pa. *Penny* did it," I croak. "I just held on." My arms are trembling from the strain. My feet and fingers are bloody. Pa sets me on the ground, and I swoon like a lady.

Catching me from behind, Jackson swings me in a hug. "You did it, boy!" he cackles gleefully. "Won me good money, too."

When he sets me down, I stare at his arm.

"That blacksmith's a wonder. My arm's almost healed!" Laughing, he holds up his wrapped elbow. I glance at him and Pa. They're both grinning, and I know Jackson's arm was never broken. But then the stewards sweep Jackson, Tenpenny, and me toward the judges' stand. The crowd cheers as Tenpenny walks past the grandstand. I hobble behind, each step misery. Master Giles joins us by the judges' stand, but I lose sight of Pa.

Jackson boosts me back onto Tenpenny. I flinch when my legs hit the saddle, but I ain't so whipped that I can't thrust out my chest when the Jockey Club president hands Master Giles the trophy.

Beside him, a man's writing down notes. "Mister Giles,

I'm a reporter for the *Lexington Gazette*. Can you tell me about your horse? Who's his sire?"

I grin down, waiting for him to ask me, the winning jockey, *my* name. Oh, that Annabelle will be so envious when she reads it in the paper! Only the man doesn't even glance my way.

Then Jackson leads Tenpenny and me off the track. This time, folks are cheering for me. Some run alongside, holding up money they won. Grinning, I give them a victory wave, but then I feel a rock bounce off my back. "Cheater!" an angry man yells. "I saw you whip Blue Belle!"

"Because of you my pockets are empty!" I hear another holler.

My smile disappears. A handful of men surround Tenpenny and me, their faces fierce. My blood turns icy.

Jackson scowls and tells them to get out of the way. I want to shout that I didn't cheat. But they don't care. They lost their wages and want to take it out on somebody—and that somebody is me!

CHAPTER SIX

rantic, I search for Pa or Master Giles, but neither is in sight. A man darts from the mob. Grabbing my ankle, he tries to pluck me off Tenpenny, who shies into the crowd. Two men clasp Jackson's arms behind his back, holding him. I cling to Tenpenny's mane, afraid to kick out. A white man is yanking on my leg, and no matter what I do, there will be trouble.

Suddenly, a band of soldiers pushes its way through the crowd. I recognize Private Campbell and Corporal Blue.

Private Campbell raises his rifle, and the crowd goes quiet.

"The boy and his horse won fair and square," Corporal Blue declares. "Let them go."

"No colored man tells us what to do, rifle or no," snarls the man holding my ankle. "Right?" He glances around at the mob, but his comrades are retreating.

He drops my ankle, then backs off, too. "No harm intended," he mutters and hurries after the others.

"You all right, Gabriel?" Corporal Blue asks.

"Yes sir, th-thanks to you and your men."

"It was the least we could do," says Private Campbell, lowering his weapon. "You and that horse made Company H a peck of money." Staying a safe distance from Tenpenny, he adds with a chuckle, "Just don't tell that white man my rifle ain't loaded."

I introduce the soldiers to Jackson, who gets to talking with them about the race. I jump off Tenpenny and pull the reins over his head. I'm bone-weary, and the colt needs tending.

As I near the stall, I hunt for Pa, wondering why he's not outside with a bucket of water. Renny is there instead. The team and wagon are waiting at the end of the barn.

"Where's Pa?" I ask.

Renny shrugs. "Your pa's got business in town. Come on, let's get that horse cooled. We're heading home tonight."

"Tonight? But Penny just raced four miles."

"Then a walk will keep him from stiffening up. 'Sides, it's Master Giles's orders. He got news that Captain Parmer and his band were leaving Versailles. He wants to git home in case they's headed to Woodville to do some mischief."

Quickly I untack the colt. While I wash him, he eats his warm mash. Later, when I rub him dry, he sighs with contentment.

By the time Master Giles comes by, it's long past noon. Mister Ham, Beale, and Henry ride up while Renny and I are loading the wagon with the last of the supplies. Jackson arrives soon after, sporting a new red cap. Pa's not with him. I lead Tenpenny from the stall.

"Let's not tarry," Master says as he snaps shut the case of his pocket watch. "Ride in the wagon, Gabriel. Henry will lead Tenpenny home."

"Yes sir." I hand the lead rope to Henry and climb in the wagon bed with Jackson. My feet and fingers are scabby, my body aches, and I'm grateful to stretch out on the feed sacks.

The wagon lurches forward, and we set off. Mister Ham and Beale ride in front. Henry follows the wagon, leading Tenpenny. The last race is over, and folks are heading for their carriages.

Jackson pulls out a small bag from under his vest. With a wink, he hands it to me. My eyes widen when I look inside. There are licorice twists, peppermint sticks, taffy, and gumdrops.

Grinning, I pull out a licorice twist and bite off a hunk before handing back the bag. *Um-um.* I smack my lips. Candy's about as close to heaven as a boy can get.

As we pass through Lexington, I keep expecting Pa to run from one of the stores. When he doesn't, my gut tightens with worry. The wagon creaks and sways, and Jackson's eyes are closed like he's asleep.

"Jackson." I nudge him with my elbow. "Where's Pa? Why ain't he with us?"

Jackson mumbles but keeps his eyes shut. Frustrated, I kneel on the sacks. The city buildings are falling behind us, and we're headed out of town.

Where's Pa?

Gingerly, I tap Master Giles on his sleeve. "Excuse me, sir. I don't aim to pester you, but I'm right worried about Pa.

Last I saw him was by the judges' stand."

Slowly Master Giles turns. He clears his throat but won't meet my eye. Renny clucks to make the team trot faster. Jackson's opened his eyes, but his gaze is directed at the countryside, not at me. I glance at Henry, who's riding close behind. Immediately he looks away, too.

I clutch the back of the wagon seat, knowing something ain't right. "Master Giles, please, sir—*where's my pa?*"

"Gabriel, you rode a fine race today," Master Giles replies.

I blink hard, wondering what the race has to do with Pa.

"Your father was mighty proud of you. He knows you're almost a man. He knows you can care for your mother while he's gone."

"While he's gone?" I repeat. "Gone where?"

"Your father stayed in Lexington. He's enlisted in the Union army." Master Giles places his hand gently on my shoulder. "He won't be coming home with us."

I stare at him like he's gone crazy. Pa's lived at Woodville with Ma and me since the day I was born. How can he not be coming home?

"That can't be," I whisper.

Then it all makes sense: Ma weeping when we left Woodville Farm. Pa telling me he loved me with tears in his eyes.

I flop down on the feed sacks. I want to cry, but the tears don't come. All I can think is *Why didn't he say goodbye?*

Jackson pulls a piece of taffy from the bag and hands it to me. "Your pa is a brave man, Gabriel. Only he ain't brave enough to bear your sorrow. That's why he didn't say goodbye. Your ma 'bout broke his heart with her weeping."

"But Jackson, that ain't fair. *I* didn't get to tell him goodbye!" I push the taffy away. Hot tears stream down my cheeks. "What if I never see him again? What if a Rebel shoots him dead?"

"Oh, you'll see him again. I'll make sure of it. I 'spect he's going to Camp Nelson for training before the army lets him loose on those Rebels. The camp's a long walk, but I'll take you there one day."

"Promise?" I dry my cheeks on my sleeve.

"Promise."

The promise makes me feel a speck better. "But, Jackson, why'd he leave me and Ma? Why'd he enlist?"

Jackson shrugs. Pulling his cap over his eyes, he slides down on the feed sacks. "He's got reasons. Your ma will tell you."

I blow out my breath. *Pa's in the army.* I picture the colored soldiers standing up to those white men, and pride slowly replaces my sorrow. Sure, I'm plum mad Pa didn't say goodbye, but next time I see him, he'll be wearing blue and fighting for freedom.

Suddenly exhaustion hits me, and my eyes drift shut. Beside me, Jackson begins to snore. Curling up on the sacks, I dream about my first trip to Lexington: One Arm, city streets, Union soldiers, licorice twists, Pa enlisting.

Then I dream about the wind on my cheeks as Tenpenny and I race down the homestretch and cross the finish line. Ma will be so proud of me that her sadness about Pa will wash away.

★★★

It's night by the time we arrive home, and I finish bedding down Tenpenny. I can barely put one foot in front of the other, but I finally make it back to our cabin. After the city, it seems tiny. Our home ain't fancy like a Lexington hotel, but Pa's job as trainer affords us better quarters than the field hands. We've two rooms and our own privy. Ma and Pa have a feather-stuffed mattress, and I have a bed to myself.

Ma lights a candle, and shadows dance on the white-washed plank walls. She sits me down on a stool in the bedroom and smoothes ointment on my blistered hands. She cocks her head, listening closely as I tell the tale of my trip.

"One Arm and his raiders had his sights on Penny, Ma, but I was fixing to get away." My voice rises. "There's no way I'd let a renegade take my horse."

Ma glances worriedly at the cabin's shut door. "Hush now. Don't talk of One Arm. News has it that this morning he passed Woodville by. Next time the farm might not be so lucky."

"Next time One Arm might not be so lucky. He might come face to face with a colored soldier like Pa. You should have seen those white men at the racetrack turn tail and run from Private Campbell and Corporal Blue." I shake my head. "I never thought I'd see the day. I can't wait until I enlist and fight alongside Pa."

"Oh, no. Don't *you* be getting any bold ideas." Ma wraps a strip of clean rag round my palm and knots it. "Your pa leaving is hard enough."

"No ma'am. I ain't ready yet. But I reckon I will one day soon. First I gotta win some more races. Might be by that time Pa will have stripes like Corporal Blue. And he'll have his own company. You'll be so proud."

Ma sighs like proud ain't what she's thinking about. She picks up my other hand. "I just pray your pa stays safe. Now, tell me 'bout the race."

Happily, I tell her the whole story, from the time Jackson pretended to hurt his arm to the end. "When I spied that grandstand, I hunkered on Tenpenny's neck, made a kissing noise, and *whoosh,* he flew like the wind across the finish line lengths ahead! Why, you should have seen me struttin' to that judges' stand."

She laughs. "That's some tale, Gabriel Alexander. It's good Jackson told me the real story."

"Well, maybe Penny didn't exactly *whoosh* like the wind." Grinning, I tip my chin high. "I bet you and Annabelle even read 'bout me in the *Lexington Observer.*"

Smiling in the flickering candlelight, Ma holds my bandaged hands in hers. "Your pa always says you have the gift, Gabriel. Use it smart. Your pa's skill with horses brought him to Woodville Farm, where life's been good to us."

"Then why'd he enlist, Ma?" Angry, I pull my hands from her grasp and jump off the stool. Suddenly, missing Pa gets the better of being proud of him. "He should be here training horses. He should be here with *us.*"

Rising from the bed, Ma sets the ointment on her dresser. When she turns toward me, tears shine in her eyes. "Your pa did it for us, Gabriel. You know he's been saving money to buy our freedom. When he heard the Yankees were paying three hundred dollars to every man who enlisted in the Union army, he jumped at the chance."

She dabs her eyes with the edge of her apron, then lays her palm below her apron ties. "Gabriel. I'm going to have a baby."

My jaw falls slack. "A baby?"

Ma's eyes gleam. "Yes. Before your pa left, he added the three-hundred-dollar enlistment fee to the money he's saved training horses. Gabriel, he bought my freedom from Master Giles. Now this child I'm carrying will be born free!"

Free! The word rings like music in my ears. I hug her round her waist. Then I rear back, embarrassed. A winning jockey doesn't hug his mama, especially when she's with child. "I forgive Pa then. Now you don't have to take orders from *no* one."

"Mister Giles will still be my boss. But he says he'll pay me wages to care for Mistress Jane."

I frown. "Why you want to keep taking care of her? You could go off and work in some fancy Lexington store. Sell flowery hats."

"That sounds like a fine dream, and maybe one day I will. For now, Mistress Jane needs me, and I need the wages. Together your pa and I will save up for *your* freedom."

"If I enlist like Pa, I can be free tomorrow."

Ma's smile hardens into a frown. "No, Gabriel. You're too young to enlist. And if I have my way, you'll never be a soldier. I won't have both my men gone. I won't have you both shot by Rebel soldiers."

"But I want to be free *now*, Ma. Like you and Pa."

"Then stay here and jockey horses for Master Giles." Ma places her hands on my shoulders. "Save your winnings. Horses helped buy my freedom and the freedom of this new babe, and one day, Gabriel, they'll buy your freedom, too."

CHAPTER SEVEN

Aristo's stall stinks. Leaning on the handle of my pitchfork, I stare at the piles of manure and sloppy wet straw. For the past two days it's rained, and the horses have been shut up in the barn. This morning, when the sun poked through the clouds, Jase, Tandy, and me hurriedly turned the horses out. Now we got all these dirty stalls to clean.

"Seven days ago, I was a winning jockey. Today I'm pitchin' manure," I mutter as I fork up a heavy mat of straw. I toss it into the wheelbarrow, barely missing Jackson, who prances backward like a sissy.

"Boy, don't be getting my britches messy." Scowling, he swats at his pants legs. He's wearing his new cap and a wool vest. A watch chain hangs from the vest pocket and a stalk of straw dangles from the side of his mouth.

I snort. "You getting as prissy as Annabelle. Weren't that long ago *you* was cleaning stalls."

"Yup, now I'm a fancy-riding free man."

A year ago, Jackson used purse winnings to buy his

freedom from Master Giles. Now, if he pleases, he can ride for other Thoroughbred owners in the area.

Jackson reaches back and pulls a rolled-up newspaper from his waistband. "Last Saturday's race is written up in here. Annabelle read it to me. There's lots 'bout Tenpenny."

"There is?" Eyes wide, I lean on the handle of the pitchfork.

Mister Winston Giles's colt Tenpenny leads down the stretch with no sign of tiring, Jackson recites from memory.

"What'd they write 'bout *me?*" I grin, picturing Annabelle's surprised expression when she read my name.

"Well..." Jackson spits out the stalk of straw.

Hanging my head, I start pitching manure again.

"Gabriel," Jackson says, "reporters don't write *my* name, and I've been winning for two years. Reporters write 'Mister Giles's colored rider' or 'the darky rider.'" He points the rolled-up paper at me. "Gotta head north if I want folks to read 'Jackson' in the paper."

"That ain't fair," I grumble.

"Well, I ain't lettin' it get to me, and you shouldn't either. You keep riding as good as you did last Saturday, and maybe one day, when the Yankees free the blacks, they'll write *both* our names."

That cheers me a speck. "You reckon I'll be racing more horses for Master Giles?"

"Ain't Mister Giles put you on more horses this week?"

I nod. "I've been galloping Captain Conrad and Savannah, and yesterday I started Penny back to work."

Crossing his arms, Jackson grins slyly. "Sounds like Mister

Giles is getting his horses ready for another big meet in Lexington. Sounds like he might let you jockey one of them."

"He is? He might? When? Where?"

Jackson chuckles. "Kentucky Association track is having a meet two Saturdays from now. Mister Giles is talking about taking a herd of horses. I'm contracted to ride some for Major Wiley, so I can't ride them all."

"I'll ride!" I prop the pitchfork against the wall, all thoughts of stall mucking banished from my mind. "And this time I'll have a pair of gloves and riding boots."

Jackson arches one brow. "You'd best get in good with the new trainer before you start making big plans."

I know Jackson's right. Just yesterday, Master Giles rode over to the Midway depot to pick up the man he hired from the North to replace Pa. But I'm not worried about making a good impression on the new trainer. "I will," I tell Jackson. "He'll think I'm the finest rider in Kentucky. 'Cept for *you*," I add with a laugh.

"Get him to put you on Tenpenny again. If you win, Mister Giles might even slip you some purse money. So think on *that*, Gabriel." Smacking the paper against his palm, he saunters down the barn aisle.

I don't have to think on it long. Purse money means freedom!

Then I scowl, wondering what good freedom would do me. Freedom sure ain't changed Ma's life. She's still fetching and doing for Mistress Jane like before. And didn't Corporal Blue say the colored soldiers are digging latrines and chopping wood for the white soldiers? Free jockeys like Jackson don't even get their names in the papers. The reporters write Tenpenny's name and he's only won one race. Jackson's won more than I can count.

Sighing, I pick up the pitchfork. Freedom sure is all jangled up. When I look at it one way, freedom don't seem so powerful. Yet then I look another way, why, it's *everything* powerful.

"New trainer's comin'! New trainer's comin'!" Jase thumps on the side of the stall as he runs down the aisle.

Dropping the pitchfork again, I jump over the wheelbarrow handles and run after him. The carriage is rumbling up the drive past the Main House. Jase, Tandy, and me watch from the doorway of the barn. Jase is little like me. He exercises the quieter horses, but one day he'll jockey, too. Tandy's already too heavy, but he's good with the two-year-olds and shines them up real pretty.

Across the way, Cato and the other workers appear in the doorway of the carriage and riding horse barn, and Oliver and his men line up in front of the mare and foal barn. Everyone knows no one can take Pa's place, but we're all wondering about the new trainer.

Renny halts the carriage in the area in front of the three barns. A white boy's sitting on the driver's seat next to him. The boy is older than me by a few years, but hard life is etched in his face. Renny jumps down and opens the carriage door, and Master Giles climbs out, followed by a whip-thin man with a bushy moustache.

"You think that's him?" Jase whispers.

Tandy nods. "I 'spect so. But who's dat white boy with Renny?"

The boy jumps from the carriage seat, and Master Giles waves us over. Me, Jase, Tandy, and the others walk toward them, and Master introduces the new man. "This is Mister Newcastle, Woodville's new trainer. He has many years of experience, and in my absence, you'll follow his orders."

Walking back and forth in front of us, Mister Newcastle inspects us like we're cattle. Then he stops beside Master and says real loud, "I've never worked with slaves before, but I've heard they're lazy and need a firm hand."

"The men and boys under you are hardworking and talented. Cato and Oliver handle the workers in the other barns. You won't have any problem." Master gestures for the white boy to step forward. "And this is Danny Flanagan, Mister Newcastle's jockey. He's all the way from Ireland to ride our horses."

My jaw drops. *Jockey?* Woodville doesn't need a jockey. Jackson and me ride Master's horses!

I glance over my shoulder. Jackson is standing in the doorway of the training barn, half-hidden by the shadows. But I know he's heard. He's furiously wiggling a stalk of straw in his mouth, and his eyes are cold beneath his cap. Abruptly he vanishes into the barn.

I turn back to stare at the boy. Only now I realize Flanagan isn't a boy. He's a man, but stunted like corn in a dry summer. A scar slices one reddish brow, and disdain fills his ghost-pale eyes.

Panic grips my innards. A minute ago, I was dreaming

about racing and freedom. But now an Irish jockey's come to Woodville Farm, and those dreams seem as far away as my pa.

★★★

In the middle of the fenced circle, Aristo shakes his head at me. Spinning, he paws the ground. I laugh at his meanness 'cause I know he's only playing.

I cluck and he trots off, circling me. No lines hold him; I keep him trotting with my voice. Pa's idea. "Teach him to trust you on the ground, and he'll trust you on his back."

Since Newcastle, the new trainer, came three days ago, I miss my pa with a heavy sorrow.

"Whoa, 'Risto." The colt walks over and nuzzles my pocket for a sugar lump. I hold out one in my palm, and while he crunches it, I watch Flanagan gallop Arrow on Master's grassy track. He rides upright with long stirrups, and he's hauling on the reins.

I grit my teeth. Arrow's throwing his head, trying to get away from Flanagan's harsh hands. Yesterday, the man galloped Sympathy, and the poor filly's mouth was bruised from his rough handling. I shake my head. If Pa was here, he'd have Flanagan cleaning stalls, not riding. How can Master not see that his horses don't like the new jockey's ways?

Ever since Flanagan showed up, Jackson's been gone. For the past three days, he's been riding horses at the neighboring farm. Newcastle has Flanagan galloping all Woodville's horses, which means the Irish jockey, *not me,* will be riding in the Lexington races.

Feels like a stone in my craw.

"Be glad that man ain't on your back," I tell Aristo as I walk over to the fence. The colt follows happily until I pull a saddle off the rail. Then he skitters away.

I roll my eyes. Aristo's a devil when it comes to the saddle and girth. Every day I rub him with all sorts of rags and blankets. I flap them in his face and under his belly, and he stands like a plow horse. But show that colt a saddle and—

"Boy! *You*, colored boy."

I tense. Newcastle's outside the fence, calling me like I'm a dog with no name. Aristo bolts to the farthest corner. He doesn't like the new trainer either.

Slowly I face Newcastle, keeping my gaze on my toes so he can't accuse me of sassing him. "Yes sir."

"Who told you to work that colt in here?"

"Master Giles, sir. He gave me freedom to train Aristo."

"Well, Master Giles isn't here this morning, so you best follow my orders. Put a halter and rope on that colt and bring him into the barn."

"Yes sir." Newcastle leaves, and I dare raise my eyes. I let out a shaky breath, afraid for Aristo. Yesterday, when Newcastle tried to go into Aristo's stall, the colt struck at him. Newcastle has hard ways with horses, and now that Master's gone, I fear the colt's going to pay.

I halter Aristo, taking my time. When I lead the colt into the barn, Newcastle's in the middle of the aisle, whip in hand. I stop in my tracks.

"Put him in his stall," Newcastle commands.

I can't move. Or speak. The sight of that whip has tied my tongue.

He whacks the handle on his palm, and Aristo slides backwards.

"Sir," I croak, "this colt don't need the lash."

"The colt *needs* the whip. Tried to strike me yesterday. Pain will teach him respect."

"But, sir, pain will only—"

Newcastle points the whip handle at me. "Defy my orders and the lash will find *your* back."

A shiver shakes me to the core. I *can't* disobey a white boss. But I *can't* lead Aristo toward a beating. "If *you* want to beat the horse, *you* put him in his stall!" I holler, flinging the rope at Newcastle. Then I turn and fly like a coward down the aisle.

"Come back here!" Newcastle bellows, but I run faster— out the door, around the corner, and into the hay barn— where I dive into last year's mound of hay, fingers plugging my ears so I don't have to hear the crack of the whip.

CHAPTER EIGHT

Gabriel!" someone calls loudly, and Jackson walks into the barn. I burrow further into the hay, ashamed of my tears.

He comes to the edge of the pile. "Boy, you skedaddled out of the barn so fast I thought you'd be in Lexington by now."

"When it's dark, I *will* run to Lexington," I declare. "To find Pa."

He squats. "Only with you gone, Newcastle will beat Aristo every day."

"He'll beat him anyway. I can't stop him. Why doesn't Master Giles send him packing?"

"'Cause Master don't see Newcastle's mean side. That new trainer is smart enough to hide it from his boss. And I can't tell Mister Giles what I don't see. Someone else will have to tell him what's going on."

"Master won't listen to me. But he would listen to you. Why'd you leave?" I accuse, eager to blame someone else. "Why you over at Major Wiley's ridin' his horses?"

I hear a sigh. "I gotta earn a livin'." Then he adds in a softer voice, "And it might be I ain't as brave as you."

I sniffle. Hay tickles my nose. "I ain't brave. Least not brave enough to face Newcastle." I peer through the stalks at Jackson.

He shrugs. "Then he'll keep on whipping Aristo. And word is, he'll be after you next."

I bite my lip. There's nothing more to say about it 'cause I *can't* stand up to a mean white man. Not like those colored soldiers did. "What are you doing here now, Jackson? You could be at Major Wiley's where you don't have to mess with Newcastle." I know I sound ornery, but I can't help it.

"I got my reasons." Jackson stands. "Look, your ma sent me to find you. She's waitin' for us in the summer kitchen. I believe she has a surprise. So dust off the hay and don't disappoint her," he says as he leaves.

A surprise? When Jackson's footsteps grow faint, I pop my head from the hay and dry my dusty tears. *Could it be a letter from Pa?*

Scrambling to my feet, I wade through the hay and peek out the doorway. There's no sign of Newcastle. I sprint from the barn and across the hay field, leaving a trail through the high grass. I weave around the fruit trees in the orchard and dash to the front of the Main House. Old Uncle's in the yard pushing a grass mower. Master Giles had the newfangled machine sent from England, so his lawn would look as fancy as the Queen's.

Vaulting the picket fence, I trot up to Old Uncle. He's pushing the mower so slowly it appears like he's walking in place. His hair is as white as Mistress's linens, and his skin's as parched as cured tobacco. He's so old that he's forgotten his age.

"Where you going in such a fired-up hurry?" he asks me. Stopping in the shade, he dabs his wrinkled brow with a rag.

"Anything faster than a turtle is 'fired up' to you, Uncle." I nod toward the main house. "I'm headed to the summer kitchen. Ma's got a surprise."

"I'm comin' with you." He leans the mower handle against the tree trunk. "Dis hot work. 'Sides, I seen Annabelle picking blackberries in the garden." He licks his lips and a twinkle lights his rheumy eyes. "You reckon a nice berry pie could be de surprise?"

"Might be." Taking his arm, I help him up the walk. "Might be a letter from Pa."

He hands me his rag. "Best wipe dose tear streaks off before you go into de kitchen. Don't want your ma to see 'em."

Hastily, I scrub my cheeks with my sleeve.

"Dat new trainer been beatin' on you?" he asks, plucking a wisp of hay from my hair. "If so, hide in my cabin tonight, not dat hay mound. Ain't nobody find you in my cabin."

"No sir. He's beatin' on my horse."

Old Uncle grunts in disgust. "A man dat beats one of God's critters ain't a man. He's a coward."

"Then the world's full of cowards."

"Dat don't mean *you* have to be a coward," he says.

We reach the marble stairs that lead to the portico, and I steer Uncle down the brick path to the back of the house.

His steps are labored, but his voice is defiant. "Only cowards beat those that are more helpless. I've lived my life respectin' the Lord's creations, and when I die, I'll join Him in heaven," he says with conviction. "But dat wicked ol' coward Newcastle, why, he ain't never goin' to see the light of heaven."

"That don't help 'Risto now," I grumble.

"Den *you* gotta help 'Risto."

I roll my eyes. Old Uncle sounds like Jackson. Don't they know I'd help that poor horse if I could? It was all I could do to keep from leaping on Newcastle and bashing his head in. Only Pa taught me never to lay a hand on man or beast. What am I supposed to do?

Voices come from the open door of the summer kitchen, a small, slat board building behind the Main House. I haven't seen Annabelle since I been back from Lexington, but I know she's heard all about my winning the race. So when Old Uncle shuffles into the kitchen, I follow with a swagger.

The room's fire-hot and smells like fresh bread. Ma and Annabelle are pounding dough. Cook Nancy's pulling a warm loaf from the brick oven. Jackson's in the middle, sitting court, his legs stretched out in front of him.

"Why, we jest in time." Old Uncle sniffs the air. "Smells like Christmas in here."

Annabelle gives me a sour look. Flour covers her cheeks, chin, and hair. "Did a strutting rooster follow you in here, Old Uncle, or is that Gabriel behind you?" she asks.

"It's Gabriel, all right, the fine jockey," I brag.

"You two quit sassing each other and listen to this," Ma

says. Wiping her hands on her apron, she pulls an envelope from her pocket.

I was right. It *is* a letter from Pa!

I pull up a chair for Old Uncle and then perch on a stool. Annabelle and Cook Nancy sit at the table with Jackson. Ma stands in the center of the kitchen, clears her throat, and reads, "Dear Lucy and Gabriel, I miss you with all my being." Looking up, she grins as wide as a new moon.

I grin, too. "Ma, when did you learn to read?"

"Annabelle's been teaching me." Her cheeks redden under the splotches of flour. "'Sides, I've read that first part so many times I know it by heart. Come on, Annabelle." She gestures for Annabelle to rise. "You finish readin'. The rest of the words are too hard."

Annabelle takes the letter and begins again:

Dear Lucy and Gabriel,

I miss you with all my being. I've been at Camp Nelson for one week. It's as big as a city, with a hospital, warehouses, a blacksmith shop, and a sawmill. The camp supplies goods for the Union armies fighting in the war. Wagons travel in and out daily. I've been mustered in and will soon begin training. Barracks are crowded but the food is plentiful.

I've met so many colored recruits that I've lost count. Most are as homesick as I. Reverend Fee has been most helpful in raising spirits and writing letters, including mine to you.

I hope all is well at Woodville. Every day I pray for you, my sweet Lucy. Keep your faith that we will soon meet.

Gabriel, please forgive your father for leaving without a proper goodbye. Care for the horses as if I was there. God bless you all.

> *Your loving husband and father,*
> *Isaac Alexander*

"Oh my." Ma has tears in her eyes and she blows her nose in her apron. Cook Nancy gives a wistful sigh, and even Annabelle's eyes are misty.

The letter makes me miss Pa more than ever.

Old Uncle whaps the table with his palm. "Where dose blackberries you picked dis morning, Miss Annabelle?"

"Right here, Uncle." Annabelle spoons the berries out into wooden bowls and pours a little cream over them, then hands us each a bowl. For a few moments, my only thoughts are of sweet berries.

When Jackson eats his fill, he clears his throat. "I have an announcement, too."

I prick up my ears. Could it be news about Saturday's race?

"I'm planning on leaving Kentucky," he says. "Goin' up North."

"What?" I almost fall off my stool. "You're leaving? Jackson, you can't!"

"I don't have a choice. Mister Giles got Flanagan riding for him. There ain't enough other work at Major Wiley's. It's time to move on."

"But Jackson," I protest, "Woodville needs you. Flanagan can't ride worth a flip."

"It ain't just that, Gabriel. Sometimes a man just knows when it's time to go. 'Sides, I hear there's a resort town in New York state where horses race almost daily, even during these war times." Leaning forward in his chair, Jackson rests his elbows on his knees and goes on with his story. "A town called Saratoga, where the streets are lit with gas lamps and the hotels have five stories of rooms. All the famous jockeys like Abe Hawkins will be riding there." He straightens. "Sounds like a place where a good jockey can make his fortune. I'll leave in a couple of days."

Suddenly, the berries taste as sour as Jackson's news. I spit the last bite on the floor. "First Pa left. Now you!"

Jackson pokes at the blackberries in his bowl 'cause he can't meet my eyes.

"Now, Gabriel." Ma tries to put a comforting arm around my shoulder, but I push it away.

"Then take me with you, Jackson. I'm a good rider. I can make my fortune, too."

"You're too young, Gabriel. 'Sides, who'd care for your Ma? Who'd watch over the horses?"

I don't have an answer. My lower lip trembles. I glance around the room. Jackson, Annabelle, Ma, Cook Nancy, Old Uncle—they're all looking at me, sorrow in their eyes.

Furious, I jump off the stool. "Leave then, Jackson. *Leave!* 'Cause I don't care!" I shout. I stomp out the door and race through the kitchen garden and into the orchard. The evening sun's falling behind a cloud, casting a dusky gray light over the fields. I need another hiding place, this time to grieve. First Pa. Now Jackson. How can they just up and leave?

Head hanging, heart heavy, I aim for Old Uncle's cabin in the slave quarters where no one will find me.

★★★

Old Uncle doesn't say a word to me when he comes in. He settles into his bed, quilt pulled to his chin. When night falls, I slip from the cabin and close the door to his snores, which rattle the room like a gourd drum. It's late, and the quarters are mostly quiet. A few field hands sit on their stoops, enjoying the warm night breeze, and pipe smoke drifts through the air.

I stop for a moment, listening to their urgent whispers. It seems that Newcastle wasn't satisfied with beating Aristo. Now, whip in hand, he's out hunting for me. Silent as a thieving raccoon, I sneak from the quarters carrying a stub of candle.

I'd be safer staying in Old Uncle's Cabin, but I have to check on Aristo.

As I dart down the path, I jump at leaves rustling in the underbrush. Could be Newcastle crouched in the shadows cast by the moon. Could be the witch who leads men astray at night.

Heart thumping, I race across the hay field, palm cupping my candle flame. The training barn's dark. Jase and Tandy sleep in the stalls, so I shield the light as I tiptoe down the aisle. Stretching tall, I peer over Aristo's half door. The colt's hiding in the corner.

I make a soft kissing noise. He flicks an ear. One hind

hoof is cocked like he don't want company. I hold the candle high, trying to see how bad Newcastle hurt him.

"'Risto, it's me," I whisper as I open the stall door. I blow out the candle, afraid of setting the straw on fire. There's enough moonlight coming through the stall window to see the colt. When I step closer, he shies sideways.

"It's me, horse," I croon. Placing my palm on his neck, I scratch under his mane, then stroke him from withers to flank. He blows a happy sound, and his ears fall limp. But when I touch his chest, he shudders and moves away.

"I ain't going to hurt you. I just want to see what Newcastle's done." My fingers lightly graze his chest muscles, and I feel thin, crusted-over scars where the lash must have fallen. Newcastle's beat the horse between his front legs, hoping to hide the marks. Hate fills me. The man had no right!

A noise outside the stall makes me tense. Lantern light fills the barn, and heavy footsteps trod down the aisle. The hair prickles on the back of my neck.

Newcastle!

I swallow my fear. This time, I ain't going to run from the trainer.

This time, I'll take the lash instead of Aristo. I twine my fingers in the colt's mane, and with my back toward the door and my legs trembling, I brace myself for the first stroke of the whip.

CHAPTER NINE

Light streams into the stall. Aristo startles and blinks. Squeezing shut my eyes, I sing quietly to the colt, *"When we all meet in heaven, there is no parting there."*

"Gabriel?" Instead of a whip crack, I hear Master's voice. "What are you doing in here at this late hour?"

I look over my shoulder. He's standing in the doorway, the lantern raised. The golden light blinds me. Relief fills me, but then confusion muddles my thoughts.

If I tell Master about Newcastle, the trainer will hunt me for the rest of my days. If I don't tell him, the horses will bear the brunt of the man's meanness.

Then Aristo nuzzles my side, and I know what path I must take.

"It's 'Risto, Master. Newcastle beat him." Tugging on the colt's mane, I pull him from the corner.

"Beat him?" Master sets the lantern on the floor. "Hold him still." He approaches the colt, who eyes him warily as he bends to study the wounds.

Master straightens. He nods once, his face weary. "See to his care, Gabriel. I'll leave the lantern." He strides from the barn, his boots thudding down the dirt aisle.

"Lord forgive me, I've done it now." I flatten my palm against Aristo's neck. "When Newcastle finds out I told on him, the trainer will flog me raw," I tell the colt. "But Pa told me in his letter to care for the horses, so I gather it's my duty."

Still, the threat of a beating sends a chill up my spine. I'll have to spend my days staying clear of Newcastle.

Reaching around the doorway, I lift the halter and rope from the wooden peg. Pa always cared for the sick horses, and now Master's putting his trust in my doctoring.

"Come on. Let's get some of Pa's healing salve on those cuts." I slip on the halter and give Aristo's ears a rub. He pushes me with his nose, but I can tell the whipping has stolen some of his fire.

"Salve will heal your wounds," I promise him, but then I shake my head, knowing it will take more than salve to heal his spirit.

★★★

Early the next morning, Jackson shakes my shoulder. "Get up, boy. We're going on a journey. Mister Giles thinks it's best for you to be out of Newcastle's way for a few days," he says as he tosses my pants on the bed.

Yawning, I sit up. "A journey? Where? You taking me to Saratoga with you?"

"No, nothing like that. We're going to see your pa. I promised, didn't I?"

That snaps me awake. Tossing back the quilt, I jump from my bed and grab my pants.

When I hurry outside, shirt untucked, the team of mules is waiting in front of our cabin, already hitched. No one else is stirring yet, but Ma's filling the wagon bed with baskets of food and gifts for Pa. She kisses me goodbye and waves as we set off for Camp Nelson.

The wagon creeps down the dusty road. Every once in a while, Jackson slaps the reins on the backs of the mules, trying to move them along. By midmorning, the sun's so hot and the air's so still, the smack of the reins has no effect. Those mules aren't about to hurry.

I'm still mad at Jackson for leaving, but he *is* taking me to see Pa, so I share some of Ma's biscuits with him.

"Reckon we'll get to Camp Nelson before nightfall?" I ask, biting into one.

"I reckon we'll get there for supper," Jackson replies. He's swaying lazily on the wagon seat, enjoying the biscuit. Like me, he's wearing a straw hat to keep the sun off his face. "That is if we don't get caught by *Newcastle.*" Slanting his eyes at me, he chuckles.

I scowl. "Ain't funny. You're leaving for some fancy resort when we get back to the farm, while I have to stay and face that man every day." My anger spills out. "And one day, I'll be coming 'round a corner, and there he'll be, whip in his hand. What'll I do then?"

"Turn tail and run like a fox," Jackson says with a laugh.

"Easy for you to say," I grumble.

We ride along, silent except for chewing. Every now and then a farm wagon passes us, but we're not on a main road, so mostly we're alone. Tipping my straw hat up off my forehead, I glance around.

I'm excited that we're going to see Pa and glad to have fled Newcastle's whip, but the trip doesn't thrill me like the one to Lexington. We haven't passed a single sweet shop or fancy hotel. Just miles and miles of hard-packed dirt road bordered by thick woods or poor farmland.

"At least One Arm ain't lurking around these parts," I tell Jackson. "There aren't any railroad depots to burn or Thoroughbreds to steal."

"One Arm ain't foolish enough to travel this close to the Union soldiers at Camp Nelson, either," Jackson says. "He don't want no colored troops after him with their bayonets."

I grin. "I bet Pa's drilling right now. I can't wait to see him in his uniform! He'll look as splendid as Corporal Blue."

Jackson gestures toward the wagon bed behind him. "Grab me one of your Ma's sweet potato pies and that tin of water. I gotta eat something or I'll fall asleep on this slow journey. A mule ain't no racehorse, that's for sure."

Climbing into the back of the wagon, I rummage through the piles. Ma's packed knitted socks and enough biscuits for a company of soldiers. I pass a sweet potato pie to Jackson, who digs into it with his fingers.

"Save some for me!" I say as I scramble back onto the seat.

Finally, the mules turn south onto the Lexington and Danville Turnpike, and the way gets busier. For the next few miles, canvas-covered supply wagons rattle past, and I guess we're getting near Camp Nelson. My palms start sweating. Pa doesn't know we're coming, and I can't wait to see the surprise on his face.

Up ahead, we spy several empty wagons parked alongside the road. Then we see a cluster of raggedy tents and log shanties. Around them, black women tend fires and wash clothes like they've set up house.

As we get closer, half-naked children appear as if from nowhere. They trot alongside the wagon, asking our names. Finally, Jackson halts the mules next to a light-colored woman hoeing a meager plot of earth. A few rows of corn poke through the dirt. A bare-bottomed youngun, clinging to the woman's skirts, sways unsteadily with each thrust of his mother's arms.

"Excuse me, ma'am. Is Camp Nelson far?" Jackson asks, all polite.

Stopping her hoeing, the woman leans on the handle. Sweat drips down her cheeks, which are hollow with hunger. I glance at the boy. His saucer-round eyes stare up from a pinched face, and I can count every rib in his skinny chest.

She thrusts her chin down the road. "Just 'round the corner. You boys enlistin'?"

"No ma'am. Visitin'."

Sticking her hand in her apron pocket, she pulls out a wrinkled piece of paper. "Please then, will you take this to

Alonzo Jenkins?" Desperation rises in her voice. "Tell him there ain't no more food for his babies."

Suddenly the wagon is surrounded with women begging us to tell recruits Ames, Elijah, or Quincy that their families are starving. Jackson and I repeat names, news, and pleas for help and take a few letters. Before leaving, we pass out the rest of Ma's biscuits and sweet potato pies. When we set off, the children are fighting over the food while the women gaze forlornly after us.

I stare back at them until we round a corner, never having seen hunger like that before. Master Giles believes a working hand needs a full belly. "Those women and children are starving," I say to Jackson. "Yet it's summer, and crops alongside the road appear plentiful."

Jackson snorts. "That don't mean food is plentiful for all. If those women back there take crops from the fields, they'll be whipped for stealing. And even on a farm when there is enough food, slaves still starve. I been on places where the master eats roast chicken and ham, biscuits and bread, peaches and pies in one sitting while the slaves get nothing but cornbread and mush."

"But those women ain't slaves," I point out.

"They might be runaways," he explains with a shrug. "Women who followed their men to Camp Nelson. I don't know for sure, Gabriel. One thing I do know, though, life ain't never easy for colored folk." He winks at me. "Unless you a winning jockey in Saratoga. Then you be counting your money every night."

I face front, not wanting to talk about his leaving. Ahead

of us, two soldiers in blue uniforms guard the roadway. They raise their rifles, halting the wagon. "State your business at Camp Nelson."

Jackson pulls a letter from his pocket. "Mister Winston Giles of Woodville Farm in Woodford County, Kentucky, has sent provisions to his former employee, Isaac Alexander, who enlisted in Lexington." He nods at me. "This is Isaac's son, who's visiting his father for the day."

The soldiers don't even glance at the letter. "No coloreds allowed unless they're enlisting. Be on your way."

"I believe we'll be allowed." Jackson thrusts out the letter. "This letter is a pass, signed by Brigadier General Speed S. Fry."

The two soldiers read the pass, and then they study us like they don't know what to make of it.

"All right then." One soldier hands back the paper. "But take care of your business and leave. Colored recruits are bunking in the Soldiers' Home on your right."

"Thank you, officers." Jackson clucks to the mules, and our wagon lurches ahead.

When we're out of earshot, I whisper, "Who is Brigadier General Speed S. Fry? And how'd Master Giles get a pass?"

"He's the man in charge of the camp. Mister Giles made his acquaintance in Lexington and got him to write us this letter." Jackson chuckles. "Seems the general enjoys a good horse race and hand of poker as much as Mister Giles."

The wagon passes through a wide gap in the fortifications. To the right, I see several cannons and rifle-pits. Soldiers pace back and forth in the hot sun, manning the defensive walls.

To the left is a fancy two-story white house with columns, porches, and three chimneys. "Bet that General Fry lives there," I say.

My head swivels as we continue down the pike. All along the road are buildings: warehouses, barracks, hay sheds— even a bakery. Like Pa said in his letter: Camp Nelson's a small town!

What I don't see are any more soldiers. There's nobody, black or white, drilling or marching. Instead, bare-chested black men are sawing and hammering boards, cutting and carrying logs, and unloading barrels and sacks. Their muscles gleam with sweat, and since they aren't wearing uniforms, I gather they're laborers, not soldiers.

"Place takes a lot of workers," Jackson muses. Tugging the brim of his straw hat over his brows, he hunches his shoulders like he's trying to hide.

"'Fraid some brigadier's going to order you to dig his privy?" I tease.

With a grunt, Jackson hunches lower.

"The camp seems empty of soldiers. Must be they're off fighting," I guess. "Bet that's where Pa is. Think he'll be back in time to see us?"

"If he ain't, we'll wait."

Down the road ahead of us there's another two-story white building, but this one's shaped like a horseshoe. It's got four doors and rows and rows of windows. In the middle of the horseshoe, a smattering of colored men sits around a fountain. Others wait on porches or hang around in doorways. Most are barefoot and wear threadbare clothes. A few white men in military uniforms walk among them, writing on notepads.

Jackson halts the mules. "Must be the Soldiers' Home."

"Reckon those men are new recruits?"

"I reckon. Stay here. I'm going to ask about your pa."

I watch Jackson approach several men who shake their heads. Then one of the soldiers gestures around back.

Jackson climbs into the wagon.

"Well?"

"Private Alexander is in the stables. The officer says we can take the mules there for the night."

My eyes dance. "Pa's a private! Bet he's in the cavalry. Bet he's grooming his mount, getting ready to ride out to war."

Jackson laughs as he slaps the reins on the mule's backs. "Bet one boy's mighty excited to see his pa."

The mules must smell hay and water because they trot up the hill to the stable. It's painted white like the Soldiers' Home, and it's so long I can't even see the far end. "Place must hold a hundred horses," Jackson says.

When the wagon crests the hill, I count four stables, arranged like the sides of a box. The stables flank fenced enclosures filled with horses and mules.

"Have you ever seen so many horses and mules in your life?" I ask.

"There are quite a many." Jackson halts the wagon at the end of the first stable. An open doorway leads inside. "Your pa could be anywhere. Hunt for him while I unhitch our mules."

I jump from the wagon seat. My legs are stiff from riding

so long, and for a minute, I hobble like an old man. Then desire to see Pa spurs me faster. I jog up and down the dirt aisle, peering into stalls. I ask everyone I see where I can find Private Alexander. Finally, a toothless colored man points to an end stall. A wheelbarrow stands outside the open door.

Grinning from ear to ear, I race down the aisle and swing around the barrow and into the stall. Pa's forking up wet straw and manure.

When he sees me, astonishment spreads over his face. "Gabriel!" He drops the pitchfork and I jump into his arms. "What are you doing here?" he asks as he sets me down.

"Jackson and me came to visit. We brought you some clothes and supplies from Master Giles and Ma. Oh, Pa, so much has happened since you left!" In a rush of words, I tell him all about Jackson going to Saratoga, Newcastle beating Aristo, and Master sending us off for two days.

Pa looks grave when I finish. "I'm sorry my leaving caused so many problems. How's your ma?"

"She's missing you but glad to be free. Only she's working jest as hard. Harder even." I glance at the pitchfork and wheelbarrow. "Like you, Pa. How come you're cleaning stalls? Ain't you in the cavalry? Ain't you fighting for freedom?"

Pa shakes his head. He's leaner than when I last saw him, and the worry line in his forehead is deeper. "Not exactly, Gabriel. Come on, I'm 'bout done here." He sticks the pitchfork in the manure he's piled high in the wheelbarrow. "Let's find Jackson. I'll show him where to stable the mules for the night."

I walk beside him, still chattering, as he pushes the

wheelbarrow. "Why ain't you off fighting? Where are all the soldiers? Why ain't you in uniform? Where's your warhorse?"

"Slow down, boy. Let me finish my work, and I'll explain." He dumps the load on a mound outside the barn, then pushes the wheelbarrow to a supply stall.

I'm busting to hear about camp life.

Finally he begins talking as we walk down the aisle. "Camp Nelson supplies food and horses to the soldiers who are already fighting. The horses stabled in this barn are broken-down remounts. My job's to get them fit for service again."

"You mean you're not a soldier?"

"I am a soldier, but even soldiers have work duties. I was lucky to be assigned to the stables. I could be digging ditches or building walls like most of the colored recruits."

"You mean until you fight, right?"

"Right. Although when I first arrived, we almost had a run-in with John Hunt Morgan." Pa's eyes twinkle.

I suck in my breath. "The Rebel leader?"

"Yup. Seems he escaped from prison. All the colored recruits were given rifles and sent to Fort Nelson or Fort Jackson to defend the camp." Pa chuckles. "Mind you, none of us had drilled with a rifle so it's a wonder we didn't shoot off our feet. It's good Morgan and his band never showed."

"That's only 'cause you scared them away."

"I doubt that. But since then the colored soldiers have been laborers. A war takes a lot of work and supplies, Gabriel."

He must see the disappointment in my face, because he quickly adds, "Things 'bout to change, though. A colonel named Sedgwick was appointed to organize the colored troops. Why, black men pour into camp every day to enlist, mostly slaves hoping to find freedom. It's a wonderful thing to behold."

I nod, remembering Corporal Blue and Company H. "Soon you'll be fighting Rebels, too," I tell him.

We leave the barn and find Jackson by the wagon. The two men slap each other's backs. We show Pa the supplies Ma sent and then bed down the mules. A white soldier with stripes on his uniform dismisses Pa and the other stable hands, and we file to the mess hall.

My stomach's rumbling with hunger, and I stand in line with the others. I take a tin plate and hold it out to a man who serves up potatoes, gravy, and greasy pork, then I follow Pa to a long plank table. I slide next to him on a rough-hewn bench. Jackson sits across from us. We're elbow to elbow with soldiers.

"This mess hall needs Cook Nancy," I say as I fight to cut the gristly pork. "Be thankful we got vittles," Pa says. "Before Colonel Sedgwick came, food for colored recruits was sparse. And if it wasn't for Mr. Butler of the Sanitary Commission, we'd be eating boot leather and sleeping under the stars."

"Why don't they treat you better?" Jackson asks. He points his fork at the men around the table. "These are fine-looking soldiers."

"Many of the white soldiers don't want negroes in Camp Nelson," Pa explains.

Jackson snorts. "You'd think the Yankees would want any able-bodied man that could hold a rifle or a shovel."

"They do. Runaway slaves are coming in droves to the camp. Even though it can be risky." Pa nods toward a burly black man shoveling food into his mouth. "Thomas over there ran off from a farm in Jessamine County. His master was so furious that he beat Thomas's wife and children, then turned them off the farm to fend for themselves. Every day, I hear hard-life stories like that."

Hard life reminds Jackson of the letters, and he pulls them from his vest pocket. "There's a whole passel of women and children waiting outside the gates," he tells Pa. "They asked us to take news to their men."

Pa takes the letters and shuffles through them. "For a while the army let the families into the camp. They lived in shanties and tents by the commissary warehouse. But there got to be too many. The guards were ordered to raze the shanties and escort the families beyond the picket lines. Now orders say everyone who ain't a recruit gets thrown out of camp. That includes women and children."

Holding up the letters, Pa stands and starts calling out names. The soldiers eagerly come over to our table to hear the news we have to share about their wives and babies. Since most can't read, they tuck any letters into their pockets. "Take them to Reverend Fee," Pa says. "He'll read them to you."

When we finish eating, men up and down the benches swap tales of running off and enlisting as they pick food from their teeth with sharpened twigs. I drink in their stories, until slowly my eyelids droop.

Pa puts his arm around my shoulders. Leaning against him, I breathe in the comforting smell of horses, and soon the drone of voices lulls me to sleep.

***

Crack, crack, crack! Shots wake me.

I bolt upright, blinking in the dark.

The gray light of dawn is creeping through the glass panes of a lone window. I'm in a narrow bunk squeezed against the wall. Pa's beside me, and I remember I'm at Camp Nelson.

Crack, crack!

Rifle shots! They can only mean one thing!

"Pa." Furiously, I shake his shoulder, trying to roust him. "Wake up. Muster the men. Camp Nelson's under attack!"

CHAPTER TEN

rack! Crack! Crack! The shots come faster. Throwing back the blanket, I scramble over Pa and out of bed, stepping on someone's arm. The room is piled with men sleeping two to a bunk and in blanket-wrapped rows on the floor.

"Hurry. We gotta find Jackson," I tell Pa as I frantically hunt for my britches, which he must have pulled off before putting me to bed.

With a groan, Pa rolls over and throws his arm over his eyes. "Hush, Gabriel, before you wake the others. We ain't being attacked. Those are Yankee rifles ringing in the Fourth of July."

"What're you talking about?" Kneeling on the floor, I search under the bunk.

"Independence Day."

I know little of Independence Day. Since Master Giles is British, we don't celebrate on the farm.

Sitting up, Pa glances down at me and chuckles. "Boy, how you expecting to fight Rebels with no britches?"

I flush mightily, embarrassed by my nakedness and stupidity. Still chuckling, Pa pulls my britches and a small haversack from under his pillow. "I believe this is what you're hunting for." He tosses the pants to me. "Let's get washed up."

By now, the men are stirring, and the bunkroom is pungent with the smell of dirty bodies. Tying my waist rope, I hurry after Pa. He's buttoning the coat of his uniform as he heads down a hallway to the washroom where a pump brings water into an indoor sink.

"Master Giles needs one of these things." I move the handle up and down. "Sure save a lot of bucket-carrying from the well." I bend and peer at the water pouring from the spout. "Where's it coming from?"

Pa splashes his face. "Long pipes run all the way to the Kentucky River."

I splash water on my face, too, then scrub myself with a rag and small chunk of soap. The rinse water dripping into the sink is gray with yesterday's dirt. "So where'd Jackson sleep?"

"In the wagon bed. He said there were too many men bunked in one room for his liking. He'll have the team hitched and ready to go after breakfast."

I stop scrubbing. "Go? We just got here."

Pa dries his face with a rag. "That pass signed by General Fry only allows you one day in camp."

"But I ain't ready to leave," I protest. "If I enlist, can I stay with you?"

"You can't enlist, Gabriel. You can't stay," he says flatly. Tossing me the rag, he hurries from the washroom.

"But, Pa!" Hastily I dry my face, tears pricking my eyes at the thought of leaving him. A bear of a man pushes past, knocking me against the wall. I hang the rag on a peg and slither past him and into the hall. It's teeming with black men of all sizes. A few are about my height, so I know I can pass for older. I'll enlist today, and Pa can't deny me!

In the bunkroom, Pa's tidying up around his bed.

"I want to stay with you," I say, trying to keep my voice from cracking.

Pa folds the blanket. "I don't want you to leave, either. I miss you with all my heart. But these are hard times, Gabriel. We all have to do what's best." He looks down at me. "And what's best for you is staying on the farm—no matter how much you hate Newcastle—and caring for your ma. Besides, you'd have to lie to pass for older. That's no way to start army life."

I raise my eyes to his. Pa's brows are pulled into a frown, so I know he ain't going to change his mind. "Yes sir," I say reluctantly.

A bugle blares from below.

"Time to eat," Pa says. "Before you leave, I'll show you and Jackson 'round the stable."

Shoulders slumped, I follow Pa, the recruits, and the enlisted men to the mess hall, where we find Jackson holding out his plate for doughy griddlecakes. But there's creamy butter and sweet molasses, and I fork down a stack despite my sadness at leaving Pa.

When we're finished, Jackson and me go with Pa and his squad to the stables. A white corporal leads us up the hill.

Once we're at the stables, the workers receive their orders and break off. We follow Pa to the barn where I found him yesterday.

"We're each assigned stalls of horses," he explains to us. "I've got a sorry bunch from a cavalry regiment that fought in Tennessee. Soldiers rode them hard and fed them harder. The forage last winter was mighty poor, and many animals gave out."

As soon as he starts talking about horses, Pa's worry lines disappear. He opens a stall door. A handsome bay greets him, and Pa pats his neck fondly. "Horses have numbers, not names. Number eighteen here had saddle sores and hoof-rot. He's 'bout healed."

He opens the door to the second stall. "This is number fourteen. His injury is going to take more time."

I go inside. A sorry-looking chestnut stares from the corner. Scars mark his withers and a wound oozes on his neck.

"Number fourteen was shot in battle. He was lucky to make it out alive." Pa shakes his head sadly. "Like soldiers, horses are dying on the battlefield."

"Only they didn't choose to fight," Jackson says. "And they sure didn't get no enlistment fee."

I scratch number fourteen under his mane. I never thought about horses dying in battle without any choice— or glory.

Pa's kept the wound open so the sickness can drain out. "Did you tell the Yankees about your healing salves?" I ask him.

Pa shakes his head. "Most of the Northerners I've talked to are city boys who don't care beans about horses. They think they're only for riding into battle or pulling cannons and wagons without mercy. At least the camp has a good veterinarian."

"You know more than that veterinarian," I brag. "Tell him 'bout your salves."

Pa shrugs. "He don't care. He's got his own way of healing. But I have suggested some changes to Captain Waite. He's one of the few cavalry officers interested in the horses' care. I told him we should turn out the remounts on cool nights so they can graze and keep them in during the heat of the day when the flies are pesky. He agreed, and since then they've recovered faster. I believe the captain's a good man, but still I need to tread carefully. Most officers don't want advice from a colored man."

Jackson makes a noise in his throat. "Seems to me *you* should be captain of the stable, not some Yankee."

"Might be that Colonel Sedgwick will make you a captain—right, Pa?" I ask. He doesn't answer, and as we leave the barn, his face gets a tight look. My gut gets tight, too, 'cause it's time to say goodbye.

We hitch the mules, and then Pa holds me close. "Say hi to your ma for me," he whispers, his voice husky. "Watch over her and that new babe she's carrying. And Gabriel, keep riding and caring for the horses."

I nod, my own throat too clogged to reply.

Moments later, Jackson whistles and slaps at the mules, and the wagon rattles down the hill toward the pike. I wave to Pa until he's a blue speck. My heart aches, but I don't want to cry in front of Jackson.

Our wagon bed is filled with packages, notes, and coins to give to the families outside the camp. When we pass a sutler's wagon, Jackson halts the mules. Using his own money, he buys overpriced tins of potted meat, cans of Borden's condensed milk, and a dozen molasses cookies. Then we drive out Camp Nelson's gates, passing the guards along the picket line. Jackson salutes them, but they stare straight ahead, their backs as straight as fence posts.

As the wagon heads from camp, Jackson whistles. "Lookee there, Gabriel."

A hundred or so black men are walking toward us down the road. They're wearing tattered clothes and carrying bundles.

"They must be recruits," I tell him. "Pa says more are coming into camp every day."

Jackson halts the wagon, and the men pass us by. They nod tiredly, and we wish them luck.

Suddenly a carriage pulled by a team of horses barrels down the road. Careening wildly, it flies around our wagon and the black men before rattling to a stop across the road, forming a barricade into Camp Nelson. Instantly the black men bunch together, and the guards run from their posts.

Jackson and I watch, wondering what will happen next.

The driver jumps from his seat, opens the carriage door, and helps out an elderly white woman dressed all fancy. "Stop those colored men!" she screeches. Her gloved finger points accusingly at the black men huddled in the road before her.

"Stop them this instant!" she repeats. One hand holding a parasol, the other lifting her hooped skirt, she hurries toward the guards. "I am Missus Francine Templar from Boyle County, and those two men wearing straw hats are my able-bodied slaves. They have run away from my farm and I want them returned!"

"Uh, missus, uh…we don't have the…" Flustered, the guards stammer uncertainly until a small squad of mounted soldiers trots from the camp.

"Good day, ma'am." One of the horsemen nods to the woman. "I am Lieutenant Kline. I have orders from the post commandant to escort these recruits into Camp Nelson."

"That's fine, but I demand that you leave me my slaves. Those two, Lou and Jake. I need them to bring in the harvest and plant winter wheat." She jabs her finger in their direction. "Lou, Jake! I *order* you into this carriage!"

"Ma'am. Please, *quiet,*" the lieutenant commands. Turning in the saddle, he addresses the band of recruits. "Your master or mistress's consent is not necessary for your enlistment. No one has authority to order you back to the farm. Is there a man here who desires to remain a slave?"

Black heads bob and shake, and murmuring rises from the group. "No!" they finally reply in one strong voice, weary no longer.

Furious, Missus Templar stamps one foot. The mounted soldiers rein their horses around the slaves. With the guards leading the way, the recruits march past the carriage and the enraged Missus Templar and through the gates of Camp Nelson.

"Look at that, Jackson." I nudge him. "We just saw freedom. And Pa's right: It *is* a wonderful thing to behold."

Buoyed by the sight, Jackson and me continue on our journey, stopping to hand out the goods to the families living roadside. Even though I'm sad about leaving Pa, my spirits stay high for several miles afterward. Just like on the trip to Lexington, I've seen and learned so many new things. Must be what Ma calls "growing up."

"As soon as I can, I'm enlisting," I tell Jackson. "Then I'll be free, too."

He grunts. "Boy, didn't you learn nothin' at Camp Nelson? A black soldier ain't free."

"That ain't true," I protest.

"Then why is your pa cleaning stalls for white soldiers' horses?"

"All soldiers have duties," I say, repeating Pa's words. "Pa says Colonel Sedgwick is organizing colored troops. I bet next time we see Pa, he'll be wearing a uniform with stripes on his shoulder. Already, he fought against Morgan. You watch, in no time he'll be marching to Tennessee to fight Rebels."

Jackson shakes his head. "That's foolish thinking, Gabriel, but believe what you want."

Angry at Jackson for doubting Pa, I retort, "You're just against being a soldier 'cause you're too cowardly to enlist."

Jackson tips his head sideways and studies me. I bite my

lip, sorry for my words. Jackson ain't a coward. But I can't have him speaking against Pa.

"Way I see it, most Yankees don't care if black folks are free. That ain't why they fighting this war," Jackson says solemnly, like he's thought on it awhile. "But you're right, I *am* a coward. I don't want to kill *or* die for freedom. That's why I'm leaving for Saratoga tomorrow—to find freedom my own way."

Crossing my arms against my chest, I turn away. I don't want Jackson to see the tears I suddenly can't hold back.

"I'm sorry I'm leaving you, Gabriel," Jackson adds with a sigh. "And I'm sorry your pa left. But sometimes, 'sorry' ain't enough to stop a man from what he needs to do."

CHAPTER ELEVEN

The next day Jackson is to catch the train to Saratoga, New York. Renny will drive him in the carriage to the Midway depot. Before they head off, I hide in the weeds by the river where no one will find me.

Leaving Pa was hard, but at least he's in Kentucky so I reckon I'll visit him again soon. But Jackson? I ain't *never* going to see my friend again. Now I know how Pa felt when he snuck off to enlist. Like him, I just ain't brave enough to say goodbye.

When the sun gets hot and the mosquitoes pesky, and I reckon Jackson and Renny are long gone, I climb from my hiding place along the riverbed. In the distance, I spot one of Master Giles's armed guards sitting under a tree by the bridge across the river. Since the scare with One Arm, someone patrols the pike around the clock. This sentry is sleeping, his rifle across his lap, his hat tucked over his face to keep off the flies.

I walk alongside a field of corn, colorful with field slaves plucking corn worms from the leaves. Their fingers are swollen from the stings. Their bare arms are scratched from the leaves. The sun beats on their heads, and sweat streams down their necks.

Since the war started, Master's lost many slaves. Some died from the fever. Some ran north. Some ran to enlist. Some just ran.

Master's always spouting off against slavery, yet he still owns slaves. He has so many, I don't know a lot of their names. As I walk past the pickers, they stare at me, probably wondering why a strong boy like me ain't working. If they were to ask, I'd tell them I haven't worked since I got home from Camp Nelson. I'd say that I don't care if I'm caught and whipped. Newcastle's going to whip me no matter.

Mister Yancy, the colored driver, sits in the shade of a tree, fanning himself with a wide leaf. There's a bucket of water and a dipper beside him.

"Mornin', Gabriel. Drink?" he asks.

"No sir, but I 'spect those workers are thirsty." I nod in the direction of the corn.

"I 'spect you're right," he replies, only he doesn't move to offer them any.

I continue on, not sure where I'm going. I do know where I'm *not* going. I'm not going near Newcastle or the stable even though I'm lousy with missing the horses. I know, like Pa said, that I need to care for them, but my fear of Newcastle keeps me away.

Sweet singing floats from the orchard and stops my journey. I search the grove, spotting Annabelle up in a peach tree. Her bare toes cling to a lower branch while she reaches over her head for early peaches. Her straw hat's hanging from a leafy twig; a basket is propped in the crotch of three branches.

I can't resist. I tiptoe through the grass. When I'm right beside her, I yell, "Boo!"

"Aiiieee!" Annabelle screams. She sways and starts to fall.

Grabbing her around the knees, I hold tight until she regains her balance. Her skirt bunches up, and when I let go, she reaches down and slaps me soundly.

"Gabriel Alexander, how dare you peek up my dress!" she shrieks.

"I wasn't peeking up your stupid dress! I was trying to keep you from busting open your pig head. Next time I'll let you fall."

"Next time don't sneak up on me!" For a second, she glowers down at me, and then her expression softens. She pats at her skirt, making sure it ain't hitched up. "Well, then, sorry I slapped you. I thought you weren't being a gentleman."

"Oh, like *you* such a lady." I rub my cheek.

"It was just a tiny slap. Couldn't have hurt *that* much."

"It like to've knocked my ear off," I grumble, and we both start giggling.

Annabelle passes me the basket and climbs from the tree so slowly and daintily, I have time to select a ripe peach from her basket. I take a big bite, letting the juice run down my chin.

"You could have asked permission," she says, snatching the basket from my hand. "These peaches aren't for slave boys. They're for making peach pies for Master and Mistress."

I snort and swallow the sweet flesh of the fruit. "Why don't you tell them to pick their own peaches?"

Her mouth falls open.

"Then tell them to make their own pies," I add. "I bet Mistress don't even know how to hold a rolling pin."

"Gabriel Alexander, what sassy remarks. What's gotten into you?"

"Nothin'." I toss my pit into the weeds. I wipe the juice off my chin with the back of my hand.

"Did your trip to Camp Nelson make you too big-headed to live here anymore?" Annabelle sets down the basket and pulls her hat from the branch.

"No. But it did teach me something about freedom." I pick up the basket. "Best let me carry that for you."

Again she stares at me. "You might be bigheaded, but I do believe you learned some manners on your trip."

"Naw. But my trip did show me something of the world. There's a whole lot of life beyond Woodville."

She tips her head forward and puts on her hat. "Like what?" she asks.

As we walk through the orchard, I tell her about Camp Nelson, the slaves marching to enlist, and the women outside the camp who've run away to be near their husbands. "Pa says the slaves are enlisting to find freedom."

"Sounds to me like the men who enlisted left their women and children to starve," Annabelle says.

"You sound like Jackson," I tell her. "He scoffs, saying that black men who enlist work just as hard as slaves. 'Freedom's in Saratoga,' Jackson says."

Thoughts of Jackson riding far away on the train make my stomach turn sour again.

"A fine jockey like him *will* find freedom in the North," Annabelle points out.

"Perhaps," I mutter, adding, "Ma says I'll find it here at Woodville Farm with Master's horses. She says if I keep riding, I can save my earnings and buy my freedom." I sigh heavily. "Only now that Flanagan's here, no chance I'll be Woodville's jockey." Angrily, I grab another peach. Before I can bite into it, Annabelle plucks it from my fingers and plops it back into the basket.

"Seems everybody has a different idea of freedom," she says. "If you asked *me* what freedom is, I'd say 'reading and writing'." Stopping by the gate in the kitchen garden, she turns to face me. "What do you think freedom is, Gabriel?"

I shrug, puzzled. No one's ever asked me that question. "I don't know." From an upstairs window of the Main House, I hear the tinkle of Mistress's bell, beckoning Ma.

Frowning, I kick open the gate. "I do know what freedom *ain't,*" I declare as I stride down the brick walkway. "It ain't running up and down the stairs fetching and carrying for *Mistress.* Ma is *supposed* to be free, but she's still actin' like a slave."

Annabelle darts in front me. "Gabriel Alexander, I'd like to slap you again. Don't you *ever* disrespect your ma. She's the finest, kindest woman I know."

Reaching out, she yanks the basket from my grasp and

sets it on the ground. Then she takes my hand and drags me down the walkway toward the Main House.

Annabelle's taller than me, and plenty strong. And she's so riled up there's no telling what she has in her mind to do.

"Where you taking me?" I ask.

"To show you why your ma is fetching and carrying." She pulls me into the Main House and down the hall to the slave stairway. Grabbing the side of the doorjamb, I brace myself with my free hand. "Oh, no. No, Annabelle. I ain't going upstairs."

"Yes, you are." Annabelle yanks my hand so hard my skin burns. "Or I'll tell your ma you were hiding by the river this morning, not cleaning tack in the barn like you said."

I grimace. Ma hates liars even more than gamblers and shirkers.

Letting go, I reluctantly follow Annabelle up the narrow stairs. When we reach the second floor, Annabelle puts a finger to her lips and leads me down the hall to an open doorway. She peeks into the room, then gestures for me to look, too.

Whatever it is, I don't want to see.

Annabelle aims her mad eyes at me, and I peer into Mistress Jane's bedroom. A four-poster canopy bed sits in the middle of the polished wood floor. Mosquito netting is draped from the bedposts, but I can see Mistress Jane through the gauzy material—least I *think* it's Mistress Jane. The person in the bed's so tiny, she scarcely wrinkles the sheets.

"Go on in," Annabelle whispers, giving me a push.

I stumble through the doorway. Mistress Jane's head is turned away. Her arm lying on the sheet is withered and pale. A bell sits beside her curled fingers.

"I didn't know she was so sickly," I whisper to Annabelle.

"She's going to die, Gabriel. She's rich and free, yet she's *going to die* anyway. *That's* why your ma still fetches and carries." Annabelle's voice trembles. Tears pool in her eyes as she gazes at Mistress Jane. "Not 'cause your ma's still a slave. 'Cause Mistress Jane *needs* her and because your mama has a soul."

I swallow hard, my gaze frozen on Mistress Jane, and I remember all the times Ma's been called to the slave quarters to tend the sick or deliver babies.

Annabelle blinks, and the tears trickle down her cheeks. "So if you asked your *ma* about freedom, she'd say it ain't just about leaving. It's about staying and caring for others, too."

Mistress Jane moans and I jump. Mumbling something foolish, I back out of the room, leaving Annabelle behind to grieve for her mistress.

By the time I run from the Main House, freedom's making my temples throb. Or could it be Annabelle's slap?

Old Uncle's in the kitchen garden hoeing a row of potatoes. When he spies me, he waves for me to stop. "Dat Newcastle still beatin' on your horses?" he asks.

"They *ain't my* horses, Uncle," I snap.

"You care for 'em, don't you? You luv 'em, right? Den dey your horses." He answers his own question with a satisfied nod and returns to his hoeing.

I kick the soft earth with my foot. I'm ashamed to tell Uncle I haven't seen Aristo and the other horses for three days. Though why should I worry about what an old man thinks? And why should I worry about what Ma, Pa, Annabelle, or Jackson thinks? Let them think what they want about freedom. I ain't doing what they want me to do. I ain't fetching or carrying or taking a whip for any man.

I'm going through the garden gate when Tandy comes flying down the lane from the barn, his arms flapping like a crow's wings. "Gabriel!" he calls as he runs, his words coming in gasps, "Newcastle's...going...to...Aristo...

I jog toward Tandy, meeting him halfway. Holding his stomach, he leans over and gulps air.

"Slow down and talk right, Tandy. What's this about Newcastle?"

"Newcastle's tryin' to saddle Aristo. Only Aristo's rearin' and fightin'. Newcastle tied him up and went to get his whip."

The blood rushes from my face.

"He's mad enough to kill that ornery colt. You gotta do somethin', Gabriel!"

"Me?"

"Your pa's gone. Jackson's gone. Cato, Oliver—ain't nobody wants to tangle with Newcastle."

"Where's Master Giles?"

"I don't know. Hurry, Gabriel." Turning toward the barn, he starts off like he expects me to follow.

Only I can't move.

My feet feel like they're nailed to the earth. *Aristo ain't your horse*, I tell myself. *This ain't your fight.*

"Gabriel, *come on!*"

I clench my fists. I picture Aristo hiding in the corner of his stall, his skin torn after Newcastle's whipping, and a howl rises uncontrollably in my chest. Maybe I ain't like Pa or Ma. And maybe I am a coward, but I can't let Newcastle beat Aristo any more.

I sprint after Tandy.

Newcastle has Aristo in the paddock. Cato, Oliver, and a throng of barn workers are standing outside the fence, watching nervously. Flanagan the Irish jockey is standing with them, a smug expression on his face.

I force my way through them and climb the rail. Aristo's in the middle of the paddock, his front legs splayed, his body trembling. Newcastle's strung a rope through one ring of the colt's halter, looped it around his hind pastern and back through his halter, and then tied it to a fence post like a pulley line.

Whip in hand, Newcastle's striding around the colt. The trainer's face is red with anger; his mouth is set in a grim line.

Aristo eyes him, but when the colt struggles, the rope yanks his head around and drops him onto his knees.

Newcastle raises his whip.

There's no way the horse can escape.

CHAPTER TWELVE

No-o-o!" Vaulting over the paddock fence, I charge Newcastle. The leather lash slices my arm before I knock the trainer to the ground and pummel him with my fists. Blinded by fury, I'm ready to beat his face bloody.

Hands grab me and pull me off. Newcastle jumps up, fingers probing his cut lip. I'm straining to go after him, but the workers hold me back. "No, Gabriel. No more," Cato hisses in my ear. "The man ain't worth it."

I yank myself from their grasp and run to Aristo. Tandy and Jase have the rope untied from the fence post. Aristo stands and shakes himself. I inspect the colt for cut marks.

A hand grabs my shirt and swings me around so hard, my neck snaps.

Newcastle glares down at me, hate in his eyes. "So you've finally come out of hiding, huh, boy?" he sneers. "Ready to take your punishment?"

I raise my chin. The man is a foot taller than me, with fists like bricks. He's right: I can't hide in the river weeds forever.

Stepping back, Newcastle snaps his whip. Silent as haunts, Cato, Oliver, and the others come into the enclosure and draw protectively around me. Newcastle glances at them, startled. "This ain't your fight," he tells them. "Get back to work." They don't move or speak. Their faces are expressionless, and they stand firm, shielding me.

Newcastle spits a wad of blood at their feet. Even he knows he's outnumbered. "Have it your way." He points the whip handle at my face. "But don't think you've won, boy."

Coiling the lash, he stomps from the paddock. Flanagan throws me a nasty look, then hurries after him. Only when they turn the corner of the barn do I exhale in relief.

"Ain't the end of your fight with dat man," Cato says to me. "Make sure dat horse is worth it."

Blood oozes down my arm where the lash bit into the skin. I walk over to Aristo. Jase is holding the rope. The colt knocks me with his nose as if to say it's all right.

I stroke his neck, and tears wet my eyes. Jase is staring at me, and I hide my face.

"Your arm's bleedin'," he says.

I shrug like it's no big thing.

"It's all right to cry," he tells me, adding in a low voice, "I cried when Tenpenny stepped on my toe. See?" He holds up his dirty foot and wiggles his big toe, which is blue and swollen. "Only don't tell Tandy. He'd call me a baby."

I give him a grin, but it quickly fades when I spot Master Giles walking toward us, his expression stern. With a yip, Jase scoots out of the paddock gate.

Patting Aristo, I bend to check his pastern. I'm worried

the rope's rubbed a raw spot, but mostly, I don't want to face Master Giles.

"Afternoon, Gabriel," he says, greeting me as if it's a fine day.

"Afternoon, sir." I straighten, my gaze downcast.

"How was your trip to Camp Nelson? Is the life of a soldier agreeing with your father?"

"Yes sir. He's doing fine."

"And how's the colt?" Master walks around Aristo, who shakes his head as if glad to be rid of Newcastle. "Mister Newcastle tells me he was breaking the colt to saddle. What do you think of his training methods?"

I stiffen.

Stopping on the far side of Aristo, Master studies me over the colt's rump. When I don't answer he goes on, "Newcastle reported just now that you attacked him while he was working with the colt. Mister Flanagan backs him up. They expect me to punish you severely, Gabriel. What's your side of the story?"

I hunch my shoulders.

"You will not get in trouble by answering me."

Ha. I struck a white man. That's already trouble.

Walking around the colt, Master stands in front of me. "If you won't tell me your side, you leave me no choice but to punish you." When I don't respond, he sighs. "Fine then. From now on, you'll work under Oliver in the mare and foal barn. You'll have no contact with Aristo and the other horses in training."

Snapping my chin up, I gasp. "No, Master Giles! *Don't*

take away Aristo and Penny. Don't take away jockeying!" I drape my hand over Aristo's neck, pressing myself to the colt's shoulder.

Master crosses his arms against his chest. "That's your punishment, Gabriel. *Unless* you tell me about Newcastle."

My mind's a jumble. Pa was always forthright with Master Giles, but I'm a slave and a boy, and I ain't sure I should speak my mind. Yet Master is asking me, straight out, like he really wants to know. Still my tongue's stuck to the roof of my mouth. If I tell on Newcastle, he'll kill me for sure.

"My horses are important to me, Gabriel," Master goes on. "Not only do I want them to win, but I want them treated well."

I swallow, loosen my tongue, and mumble, "Newcastle is mean, sir. He doesn't know how to train a horse like Pa."

"No trainer can replace your father, Gabriel. He's an exceptional horseman, and I miss him sorely. However, good trainers are hard to find. Newcastle came highly recommended. His methods are accepted by most trainers and owners."

Now my anger flares and I can't stop my words. "Those methods are wrong!" I blurt, twining my fingers in Aristo's mane. "A horse wins a race with *spirit*. With *heart*. If you beat out that spirit, if you break his heart, then he'll only run out of *fear*. And fear don't win races!"

A smile lifts the edges of Master's mouth. "Well, I see you do have an opinion. Now, what do you think about Flanagan, the new jockey?"

I scoff. "Man's got hands of lead. A jockey needs soft hands to talk with the horse. Flanagan's hands only say 'pain and hurt' to the horses."

"Interesting." Master taps his cheek then points his finger at me. "Tell you what. Let's put your opinions to the test. Three days from now, after noon meal, you and Flanagan will race."

At the word "race" my head snaps up.

"You on Savannah. Flanagan on Captain Conrad. Two laps around the training track. Whoever wins gets to jockey during Saturday's meet."

"Yes sir!"

"You have three days to get Savannah ready. Use those days wisely."

"I will, sir!"

"And Gabriel, rest assured, I'll see that Newcastle will no longer be using his whip on you and the horses." Master walks from the paddock, leaving me with high hopes for the first time since Newcastle and Flanagan came to Woodville. "Hear that, Aristo? I get to prove I'm the best. Then Master will get rid of Flanagan and I'll be Woodville's jockey!"

The colt drops his head to graze. My high hopes drop too when it dawns on me what Master's done. He's put me on *Savannah*.

Savannah is a flighty, three-year-old filly afraid of her own shadow. Captain Conrad's a seasoned racehorse.

Ain't no way she can win. Oh, how I wish Pa or Jackson was here to help me.

But they ain't here. It's up to me.

No, it's up to Savannah and me. Clucking to Aristo, I trot him from the paddock. There's no time to waste. For the sake of the horses, I can't let Flanagan and his heavy hands win. I can't let Newcastle and his mean ways win. If I'm to win this race, I need to get working with that filly!

★★★

"Gabriel." Ma leans over the bed and gives me a shake. "Wake up."

I groan and nestle deeper into my pillow.

"Master's sent word. He's taking Newcastle with him to town this morning."

I shoot upright, eyes crackly with sleep. "Newcastle's leavin'?"

She nods. It's half-dark, but I can see her smile. "They'll be gone for 'bout an hour. Best you get down to the barn and work that filly before Newcastle comes back." She hands me my pants and I slither into them.

When I hurry around my hanging quilt, I almost run into Annabelle, who's setting a steaming plate of cornmeal mush on the table. She greets me as if she's always in our kitchen at dawn. "Morning, Gabriel. Best eat up before you ride."

She pours honey over the mush.

Sliding onto the chair, I spoon up a heaping mouthful. "Um-um. Sure is tasty."

"Now don't be getting big ideas about me serving you every morning," Annabelle says tartly. "But your ma's feeling peaked, and Master sent me from the Main House to deliver his message."

I nod a thank-you.

She folds her arms. "Seems Master wants you winning as much as me and your mama."

I blink up at her. Ma comes from behind the hanging quilt, her arms laden with soiled bed covers. "Whole farm be placing bets," she says. "From the guards to the field slaves."

I choke down a huge bite of mush. "The whole farm?" I croak, realizing this race might be as big as Christmas.

They both nod. "So hurry and eat," Annabelle fusses. "I heard that yesterday Newcastle kept you jumping with chores so you had no time to ride Savannah. Well, last night when I was serving Master his supper I told him right out, "Master Giles, the race won't be fair if Gabriel doesn't have a chance to work with that horse. And sir, I know you're fair." She yanked the half-finished plate off the table. "So go, Gabriel, he's giving you an hour."

"Yes ma'am!" I salute Annabelle like I was Pa and she was a captain, and then dodging her kick, I run from the house.

Minutes later, I catch Savannah in her pasture and slip on the bridle. Leading her out the gate, I steer her to the mounting block and leap on. She takes off at a trot.

"Settle, settle," I croon as we canter away past the barn and into the hayfield. Her nose is high, her nostrils flared, her stride stiff. The rising sun beats on my shoulders, and soon we're both sweating.

We canter through the high grass to the river, which is

wide and sluggish. Savannah skitters to a stop at the muddy edge. She flings her head and dances nervously, the mud sucking at her hooves. I hum to her. One thing I know for certain, if we're going to beat Captain Conrad, the filly has to trust me.

A frog plops into the water. Savannah flies backward. But with hands, heels, and voice, I urge her back to the edge. She takes one tentative step into the water and then freezes, her forelegs ramrod straight. A soft wind blows from the opposite side of the river, bringing with it the sounds of blackbirds, bullfrogs, and cicadas.

It seems to take forever, but I'm patient, and finally Savannah blows out a huge sigh, drops her head, and drinks. Grinning, I lie back on her rump and close my eyes. Yesterday, Newcastle *did* run me ragged mucking stalls, scrubbing buckets, and grooming horses until he thought I was too spent to work with the filly. Meanwhile, Flanagan was taking it easy—sitting in the shade, polishing his boots, and breezing Captain Conrad in the cool of the morning.

But come evening, when Newcastle was tucking into a hearty supper, I snuck Savannah out of the stall. As the sun lowered, I led her from cornfield to wheat field. While we walked, I told her how we had to win the race. She listened, flicking her ears at the sound of my voice. By the time the sun was down, the filly's head was draped over my shoulder, and I knew she'd heard every word. Tomorrow if I have to, I'll sneak her out again. We'll canter up and down the hills, maybe stretch into a gallop, just for a beat, so she can feel what it's like to run wild and free.

After that, it's race day.

Voices make me open one eye. I peer sideways, spying two men on the bridge that crosses the river. Curious, I sit up. They're Master's armed guards, patrolling the area. Their heads are together, and I wonder what they're discussing.

Rumor's been flying through the barns that One Arm and his men are on the move again. For days, they've been holed up in some wild hollow or Rebel's farm, steering clear of the Yankees. But now, rumors say, they're out of supplies, horses, and money.

Shivering, I gather the reins and nudge Savannah from the water. I ain't got time to worry about One Arm and his band of raiders. I need to groom Savannah to a shine, then feed her a special ration of oats before Newcastle returns from his trip to town.

Winning this race won't just help the horses. It will help me on my way to freedom.

CHAPTER THIRTEEN

You goin' to win today, Gabriel," Jase says confidently as he strides down the aisle next to me. "You and Savannah will beat that Flanagan."

"I won't win wearing these boots," I grumble. "They're pinching my toes."

"So kick 'em off."

"Ma says I have to wear them. She says Pa wore them when he first started jockeying. She says they'll bring me luck."

Jase chortles. "Ain't gonna bring you luck if they hurt your feet. 'Sides, you always listen to your ma?"

I don't answer because it would make me sound like a mama's boy. When I reach Savannah's stall, I peer inside. The filly's eyes are like moons in her black face. She's pacing around the stall, kicking up straw and manure.

All this morning, curious folks have been stopping by her stall to stare. Like Annabelle said, the whole farm's making bets on this race, and Savannah's smart enough to know something's up. Something scary.

"All the barn hands are betting on Savannah to win," Jase tells me. "They say she's lightning."

I know he's lying because of his shifty eyes. "I don't care beans about the barn hands," I say, then I repeat Pa's words. "This race is about me and Savannah."

"Then you in trouble." Standing on tiptoes, he's looking over the half door into the stall. "'Cause that filly's as twitchy as a cat-cornered mouse."

Frowning, I give Jase a hard pinch on the arm.

He squeals. "What'd you pinch me for?"

"You best be rooting for *us*."

"I am."

"He'll be the *only* one rooting for you, then," someone says behind us.

Jase and I spin around. Flanagan's standing in the aisle. He's wearing shiny black boots and pure white breeches. One gloved hand grasps a riding whip, which he taps against the side of his leg. Spurs stick out from the heels of his boots.

Flanagan laughs when he sees my raggedy britches, pointy-toed boots, and homespun shirt. "See you at the finish line, laddie—*if* your horse makes it that far."

"Humph. Fancy clothes don't mean a man can ride," I mutter as he saunters down the aisle. I pull Savannah's bridle from the peg and touch the bit with my tongue, making sure Newcastle didn't smear some nasty tonic on it, then check the straps for slices in the leather. Newcastle ain't gutsy enough to defy Master and come at me with the whip. But a mean man is usually a cheating one, too.

I open the stall door. Savannah shoves her muzzle in my hand. Her ears flick like blackbird wings. Last night I slept in her stall. I wanted her to know my smell as well as her own—and besides, I didn't trust Newcastle not to tamper with the filly.

Savannah is already wearing her saddle. I put it on her first thing this morning to give her back muscles time to warm. I run my hand under the pad, hunting for burrs or prickers, and then tighten the girth.

"Saddle up!" Cato calls out.

I peer over the door and down the aisle. Newcastle and Flanagan hover outside Captain Conrad's stall while Tandy tacks up the colt for them.

Jase brings me a box. Standing on it, I bridle Savannah, humming and singing all the while. She likes "Amazing Grace" and "Lorena" the best.

"Filly ain't singing in the church choir, Gabriel," Jase grumbles.

"I'm just soothing her," I tell him. Soothing *me*, too, only I don't admit that.

"Captain's all tacked up," Jase reports from the doorway. He's hopping from one foot to the other like he's as nervous as I am. "Tandy's leading him down the aisle."

I jump off the box. "We're ready, too."

"Can I lead her?" Jase pleads.

"Not this time. Savannah knows me, Jase. To win this race, I've got to keep her trust."

"I reckon. Might be you could use this, too." He digs in

his pocket and pulls something out. He gives me a shy look, then hands me his lucky rabbit foot.

Smiling, I slip it down my right boot.

Moments later, we're walking through the gap in the fence and onto the grassy track. Field slaves and barn workers are strung along the rail like it's a holiday. Even the armed guards have quit their posts to watch. Some folks nod. Some wish me luck. I pay them no mind, all my attention on Savannah. Yesterday she cantered sweetly for me. But then the fields weren't bright and noisy with folks, and now the filly's dancing on my boot toes.

"Nothing to be scared of," I tell her.

Flanagan's already mounted on Captain Conrad. The colt's neck is arched and he's mouthing the bit, eager to get along. Savannah floats toward them, each step hesitant.

"Come on, boy, get your horse over here!" Newcastle shouts at me. "We ain't going to bite." The two men guffaw.

I look for Master Giles. He's by the finish line pole, checking his watch. "Oliver will start you," he calls. "Then go twice around."

Cato boosts me onto Savannah. I warm her up with a trot down the homestretch, and she rolls her eyes at the onlookers. Newcastle hollers to quit wasting time and get on with the race, but Master acts like he doesn't hear.

By the time we reach the starting line, Savannah's quit goggling at the crowd. Reaching down, I run my palm softly along her neck. *This is it,* I think. *This is my chance to prove that I should be Woodville's new jockey.*

ALISON HART

I perch forward, my weight in the stirrups. Before I can twine my fingers through Savannah's mane, Newcastle yells, "Go!" and smacks Captain on the rump.

The colt springs forward, Savannah right with him. Only *I'm* almost left behind. Landing hard on the saddle, I lose my right stirrup. Savannah's cantering sideways, and field hands jump out of her way. Heart thumping, I grab a handful of mane, pull myself forward, and catch my balance. Then I kick my foot out of the left stirrup. Gathering the reins, I steer her straight.

Captain Conrad's at least seven lengths ahead. His powerful hind muscles churn; his hooves kick up clods of turf.

I take deep breaths, slowing my drumming heart. Hunkering low, I jiggle the reins with my fingers so the filly can feel me. Savannah has a mouth soft as cotton. She needs reassuring, not pulling. Least that's what she told me those three days I exercised her.

"Two miles," I whisper. "There ain't no rush, Savannah."

Her stride's steady as she canters downhill. Captain Conrad's still a good distance ahead. Master's exercise track ain't like the Kentucky Association track; it's grassy hills and swells, trees and bushes. We canter through a stream, the water spraying Savannah's belly. Then the track winds back toward the barns.

Sensing home, Captain Conrad charges faster. Flanagan's standing in his stirrups, fighting him because he knows we got another mile.

I smile. Fighting taxes a horse as much as running.

We fly past the crowd, Captain Conrad ahead by five

lengths. Movement by the willow tree catches my attention. It's Ma and Annabelle waving colorful ribbons.

"Win, Gabriel!" Annabelle hollers.

We gallop away for a second lap around. The sun's high and hot, and the wind burns my cheeks. Savannah's sweaty neck shines like a polished boot, but her head's still tucked and her gait's strong, so I know she's got speed left inside. I slow her to a canter as we head up the hill from the stream. It's the last hard pull. If she can save a burst for the home-stretch, we can win.

The hill tires out Captain Conrad, and slowly we pull alongside. The colt's neck is stretched flat and his nostrils flare pink. But he's got height and muscle on the filly, and he ain't going to quit.

Flanagan ain't going to quit either.

Digging his spurs in Captain's side, he pushes the colt on. His whip hand flails up and down, and the slaps of leather on horse flesh make me wince. I steer clear, making sure he doesn't use the whip on Savannah or me.

I aim my eyes on the finish line pole.

Propping my hands higher on the filly's neck, I whisper, "Now, Savannah."

I chirp, Savannah flows into a gallop, and we pull effort-lessly past Captain Conrad. I grin, seeing that finish line ahead.

Only something is wrong.

The crowd is scattering. Cato's waving both arms. Master's running for the barn.

We thunder past the finish-line pole. By the willow tree,

121

I see Ma and Annabelle staring panic-stricken toward the Main House. As I rise in the stirrups to slow the filly, Cato's frantic shout reaches my ears. "It's One Arm and his raiders! Get the horses to the barn!"

CHAPTER FOURTEEN

The thudding of a hundred hooves on hard ground comes from the direction of the Main House. Chills prickle my arms.

I pull hard on the right rein, swinging Savannah toward the willow tree. "Get to the house. Bolt the doors!" I holler at Ma and Annabelle, and they dash off in a flurry of skirts.

Master Giles and the armed guards are hurrying toward the oncoming raiders, who jog their mounts past the house toward the barns. My heart quickens.

They're after the horses!

As I trot down the track, I lose sight of Master Giles, Cato, and Oliver. The field slaves are shooting like buckshot into the cornfield beyond the track. Flanagan jumps off Captain Conrad and yanks him toward the gap in the fence. But the colt staggers and almost falls. With a frightened glance toward the raiders, Flanagan drops the reins and runs after Newcastle, who's fleeing toward the barn.

Savannah halts behind Captain Conrad. I leap from the saddle, land on one leg, and tumble to the ground. "Jase!" I holler as I scramble to my feet. Jase worms his way through the scattering people. "Take Savannah to the barn. Untack and cool her. Tell Tandy to hustle out here with a bucket of cold water and a rag. Captain's got the shakes."

Jase runs off leading the filly.

Captain sways. Pa says the shakes happen when a horse's insides get so hot its body can't cool itself. In the distance, I hear men shouting. I see a handful of raiders in front of the carriage barn. They're dismounting and their guns are drawn.

Thoughts of One Arm make me tremble. I want to run into the corn with the field slaves, but I can't abandon Captain.

Leaving the colt, I speed down the hill toward the icehouse, which is hidden in the bank near the stream. I lift the latch and throw open the wooden door. The small room's dark and cool. Ducking inside, I kneel on the dirt floor. There's a hole in the middle of the floor. Deep in the hole, ice stays frozen most of the summer.

I uncover the hole and pull up the bucket, praying for ice, not snakes.

My hand touches a slippery chunk.

I wrap it in my shirt hem, close the door over the hole, and run back up the hill. Tandy's struggling from the barn with a bucket of water. Captain's leaning against the fence rail, his head drooping.

"Get the saddle off, Tandy. We got to cool him."

Tandy sets down the bucket. He tries to unbuckle the girth, but his fingers are shaking and he keeps looking uneasily over his shoulder.

Pulling off my shirt, I wrap the ice in it and press it against the vein in Captain's neck. "Is it truly One Arm and his raiders?" I ask, keeping my voice low.

He nods miserably. "I s-s-scared, Gabriel. I don't want to die."

"You ain't going to die. One Arm's after *horses,* not us." I peek over Captain's neck. "Where's Master Giles and Newcastle? Are they guarding the barns?"

Shrugging mutely, Tandy pulls off the saddle.

"Take the rag and wash the water over Captain's back. We got to cool him, so he can walk. Then you hide him in the icehouse. Raiders won't go there."

By the time the ice has melted, Captain's somewhat perked up. "Go, Tandy. When Captain's safely tucked away, you come back."

Tandy hurries off down the track, Captain following unsteadily behind. I doubt Tandy will come back. Later, we'll find him shivering in the icehouse with Captain Conrad and the snakes. Not that I blame him. Raiders are worse than snakes.

Pulling on my wet shirt, I sprint to the barn. The back doors are shut tight and secured from the inside. I scratch on the wood. "It's Gabriel."

I hear the board being lowered and Cato cracks open the door. I slip inside. When he shuts it behind me, I can't see.

Cato grips my shoulder. "Master's talking with One Arm," he whispers. "Two guards are posted in front of each barn, but they ain't no match for twenty-five raiders."

I know my way round the barn day or night, so I walk

down the aisle, peering into each stall. The windows are shuttered, but I can see the horses in the slivers of light. Sympathy, Arrow, and Tenpenny rustle uneasily in their stalls. Jase is rubbing down Savannah with a rag. Blind Patterson's throwing his head, confused by the sudden change in sounds. Daphne and Romance are nervously munching hay. Lastly I check on Aristo.

My heart sinks. The horse ain't been right since Newcastle tied him up, and now he's wringing wet with fear. When I open the stall door, he throws himself into a corner.

I stand quiet, waiting for the colt to see it's me. Finally he comes over and lips my hand. I stroke his sweaty neck. My throat's tight. "'Risto, I ain't going to let nothing more happen to you," I choke out. "I promise."

"Gabriel, I hid Captain like you said." Tandy's standing behind me in the stall doorway. His skinny knees are knocking together. I grin, glad he was brave enough to come back.

Loud arguing from outside makes us both start. With a moan, Tandy flattens against the doorjamb. "They's coming to get us, Gabriel."

"They ain't after *us*," I repeat, but my heart's banging, too.

I scratch under Aristo's forelock. "Be back in a jump," I whisper before leaving the stall. Tandy tags after me down the aisle.

Cato's at the front of the barn, the side of his head against the wooden door like he's listening. Flanagan's beside him, jawing a wad of tobacco. When I come up, he spits a black stream by my feet.

I ignore him. "Can you hear what they're saying, Cato?"

He motions for me to listen.

I press my ear against the wood. I can hear Master's voice. He's telling One Arm that there's no call for violence.

"Ha. Lies from a bloody Yankee," a deep voice replies. "You fly the British flag, Mister Giles, but you ain't on the side of us Rebels."

"Now, Captain Parmer, didn't I give you fair warning the other day that the Union soldiers were after you?"

"Reckon you did. But it weren't to save me. It was to save your *horse.*"

I swallow hard. One Arm hasn't forgotten about Tenpenny. If only I could see what was going on.

Then I notice a circle of light at my feet. There's a knot-hole by my knees. Stooping, I put my eye to it.

Tandy plucks at my shirt. "Can you see?" he whispers. Jase comes up the aisle, eager for a look, too. I wave them off. Master and two guards are in the middle of the circle of raiders. One Arm is still on his horse. The others have dismounted and are holding their horses, which are a sorry lot. They're so thin and spent it's a wonder they're still standing.

"You were hiding a racehorse that day, Mister Giles," One Arm continues. "Name of Tenpenny. I heard he won at the Lexington meet the next day. I figure you owe me."

"You're right, I do." Master puts his hand inside his coat. Instantly, One Arm aims his revolver. The two guards nervously raise their rifles. Twenty-four weapons cock in response, and the guards hastily drop their rifles on the ground and stick up their hands.

One Arm chuckles. "If you're thinking about reaching for a weapon, Mister Giles, I'd think again."

"No, no." Master pulls out a wallet. "I was aiming to pay you what I owe."

One Arm laughs. "Hear that, boys? He thinks we want *money*." He presses his lips into a thin smile. "Well, we *do* want money. But what we want *more* are fresh mounts. As you can see, ours are played out." Cocking his pistol, he points the barrel at Master's head. "Empty out your barns, Giles. I want those Thoroughbreds."

I stifle a gasp. *No, don't let him have the horses!*

"And what do I get in return?" Master calmly asks.

One Arm sweeps his arm in an arc. "Why, we'll swap our fine horses for yours. Seems fair."

"Your rode-to-death mounts for my purebreds?" Master shakes his head. "I doubt that's fair. I see broken knees and split hooves, and not a Thoroughbred in the bunch."

"You also see the end of my gun barrel."

"And I have armed men at every barn. There will be a fight."

"No problem." Using the butt of his gun, One Arm tips up the brim of his hat. "Corporals Keen and Hardy!" he hollers over his shoulder. A moment later, two riders trot up with burning torches. "When I count to ten, set the barns on fire."

"Stop!" Master shouts. "That won't be necessary." Shoulders slumped in resignation, he nods toward the barn that houses the carriage horses. "I'll personally escort your men into the barn and let them pick their horses."

I jump up. Tandy and Jase push each other, trying to take my place at the knothole.

"Cato, did you hear that?" I whisper excitedly. "Master's taking them to the wrong barn."

Cato nods. "Master's smart. Buying time. 'Cept those renegades know horseflesh. They ain't gonna be fooled for long."

"Long enough for us to get the Thoroughbreds to safety!"

Cato frowns.

"This is our chance to save the horses," I rush on. "You've heard the stories 'bout how the raiders ride their horses to death. We can't let that happen to Penny and 'Risto and the others. If we ride the horses from the barn, there ain't no way their mounts can catch us."

Jase and Tandy are looking up from the knothole like I'm crazy. Flanagan snorts. Even Cato shakes his head. "No suh. They ain't my horses. An' this ain't my fight."

"Tandy? Jase?"

The two slowly stand. Jase is chewing his lip and Tandy's staring glumly at his toes. Neither can even sputter a *no*.

"Flanagan?"

"Why should I care about some rich man's horses?" He shoots tobacco juice past my leg. "Mister Giles can just buy new ones." Arms crossed, he saunters down the aisle.

My fingers curl into fists. "Then I'll do it alone."

Squatting, I peer out the knothole. One Arm and a handful of his men are following Master. More than a dozen raiders still wait outside, but their attention is on the carriage barn. I can take the horses out the back door—

Only there's no way I can lead all of them.

Which one do I leave behind? Blind Patterson? He's no good to the raiders, but they might shoot him out of spite. Sweet Savannah? Tenpenny?

My temples throb. I *can't* take them all. But if I don't do something fast, *none* will be saved.

Suddenly I know what to do. I'll ride Aristo and lead Patterson and Savannah. I'll let the others free. Hopefully, they'll follow us. If we can make it across the river, we can hide in the woods.

It ain't the best plan, but at least I can try. I hurry down the aisle and grab Aristo's halter.

Jase taps my shoulder. "I'll help," he whispers.

"Me too," Tandy says behind him.

My spirits lift. We *can* try and save them all!

"Good. Now, listen carefully. Tandy, you bridle Tenpenny. You'll ride him and lead Arrow and Romance. Jase, you ride Savannah—she's still bridled—and lead Sympathy and Daphne. I'll take Aristo and Blind Patterson. We'll gallop out the back barn doors at the same time, then spread out to confuse the raiders."

The two nod eagerly.

"Tandy, you'll ride into the cornfield. Jase, you circle round toward Major Wiley's farm. I'll head to the river. If the raiders get close to you, let go of the horses you're leading and ride for your life. Got that?"

The two nod again. Grabbing bridles and halters, they dash down the aisle. Cato's in Patterson's stall putting a halter on the stallion. "I won't ride with you," he says solemnly, "but I'll help you get away."

I hurry into Aristo's stall. The colt is tense. He throws up his head, and I know I ain't going to coax the bridle on. I clip two ropes to the halter.

Clucking, I lead him out of the stall and over to the front doors of the barn. Jase is mounted on Savannah, waiting by the back doors. He's holding the leads of Sympathy and Daphne. Cato's helping Tandy climb on Tenpenny. Bending, I peer through the knothole. My pulse sets to marching double-quick.

One Arm and Master are coming out of the carriage barn, followed by a group of raiders. One Arm has a gun to Master's temple. "No more tricks, Mister Giles," One Arm is saying. "I don't want wagon horses. I want Thoroughbreds and *I want them now.*"

CHAPTER FIFTEEN

hey're coming! I snap upright. Tandy's mounted on Tenpenny and waiting in the aisle with Arrow and Romance. Savannah, Sympathy, and Daphne are skittering in front of the closed back door. Cato's leading Blind Patterson from this stall. All the horses know something is wrong. Their eyes are white in the dark and I can smell their sweat.

I say a quick prayer that this ain't the last time I see my horses.

Then I hear the jingle of spurs and the rasp of One Arm's angry voice, and I know we have to move.

Cato throws me on Aristo's back and hands me Patterson's lead rope. He runs down the aisle, lowers the board, and swings wide the rear barn doors.

"Run, Jase!" I holler, and the boy clamps his legs around Savannah's sides and the three horses streak from the barn. "Run, Tandy!"

Tandy kicks Tenpenny. Cato whoops at the colt, and Tandy canters him from the barn, leading Arrow and

Romance. Behind me, I hear cursing and the sound of an ax striking against wood.

Aristo rears. Sticking tight, I lean forward on his shoulder until he drops to the ground. Patterson's prancing in confusion, so I snug his head against my thigh and aim both horses down the aisle toward the open door.

"Go!" I cry as the ax splinters the front door behind us.

The colt leaps in the air, digs in hard with his hooves, and charges past Cato. Half-wild, he races from the barn, through the gap in the fence, and onto the grassy track. My right hand grasps his rope reins; my left arm's snapping with the pull of Patterson's lead rope.

There's no sign of Jase and Tandy, but I hear shouts from outside the barn.

"They're escaping! Mount up! After them!"

Then the wind deadens the raider's cries.

Aristo flies down the track. Patterson's following gamely alongside, but I can tell there's no way the stallion can keep up.

We canter down the hill and across the stream to the icehouse. Least Captain's safely hidden inside. A clump of pines runs along the bank, ending in thick brush. Steering with one hand, I urge Aristo deep into the pines. Boughs slash my head and whack my knees.

"Whoa." My breath comes in ragged spurts. Reaching high, I wrap Patterson's rope around a branch and knot it tight. I know he's wracked with fear. But fear's better than death.

"Hush now, Patterson," I tell him. "Don't fight the rope.

Aristo can't outrun them with you dragging behind. I'll come back for you. I *promise.*"

Moments later, Aristo and I burst from the pines. My soul leaps into my throat. Four raiders, One Arm in the lead, are swooping toward me.

I've got to lure them away from Captain and Patterson!

One Arm yells, "Get him!"

Yanking on the rein, I wheel Aristo. "Run!" I holler, but he doesn't need my command. He's ready to fly.

We race down the grassy track. Halfway round the homestretch bend, I steer Aristo sharply to the right and into the hay field that stretches to the banks of the river. As we lunge through the tall grass, I pray we miss the groundhog holes.

Full tilt, we tear across the field. Aristo gallops with abandon, like he don't even know I'm on his back. I'm hunkered so low that his windblown mane stings my cheeks. I glance over my shoulder, figuring we've left those raiders in our dirt, but the four are still in sight.

We have to make the trees on the other side of the river.

Down the bank we slide. Aristo jumps a rocky ledge and plunges into the rushing water. I cling to his back as he trots deeper, knees reaching high.

Suddenly, I hear the sharp crack of a rifle, and a piercing blast knocks me off my horse. I hit the water with a slap. Down, down I sink, the murky water pulling at my clothes and boots.

I flail my hands and legs. Searing pain shoots through my right arm.

My lungs are bursting.

My foot hits rocky bottom. I kick hard and push myself to the surface. My mouth gulps air. Quickly I wipe the water from my eyes and twist from side to side, looking for Aristo.

Up ahead, One Arm's ridden his horse into the river after the colt. The other three raiders are on the bank. One has a rifle aimed in my direction.

A blast from the gun's muzzle sends me diving under the water. I fake I'm hit, and going limp, let the current carry me away.

I float downriver and out of sight around a bend. A branch snags my shirt. Paddling toward shore, I find bottom and wade into the river weeds. My boots are heavy with water.

Sitting in the shallows, I tug them off. The rabbit's foot plops into the water. I notice blood streaming down my wet arm. My shirtsleeve's torn and there's a gash below my shoulder. But I ain't got time to rip my shirt and bandage the wound. I promised Aristo no more harm, and a boy has to keep his promises.

I fish out that rabbit's foot and tuck it into my soggy pocket. Barefoot, I sneak my way up the shoreline. When I'm closer, I wade back into the water and crouch in the weeds, making my way around the bend. One Arm is on the bank. He's got Aristo's two ropes clamped under his stump of an arm. With his good hand, he's struggling with the girth on his own horse. The other raiders are gone, probably hunting Tandy and Jase.

I could sneak up and try to wrestle Aristo away, but there's no cover. One Arm would shoot me without a thought.

Then it dawns on me what One Arm's planning: He's going to saddle Aristo and ride away on him.

I stoop low in the water, the blood from my wound swirling around me, and wait for my chance.

One Arm frees the girth and slides the saddle off his worn-out horse, which ambles off into the hay field. Then the man turns toward Aristo. The colt's already eyeing him. When One Arm goes to throw the saddle on his back, Aristo reels and the saddle drops to the ground

I dart from my hiding place, slosh through the water, and clamber up the bank. One Arm's chasing after Aristo, so he doesn't see me. He's got hold of the rope with his good hand, and he's yelling, "whoa, whoa," as if the colt's going to obey.

Throwing his head high, Aristo yanks the rope from the raider's grasp and trots in my direction. I spring forward, grab a fistful of mane, and vault onto his back. As the colt leaps up the rocky ledge, I lean down and snatch the dangling ropes.

One Arm roars in fury.

A dozen raiders are galloping down the hay field, cutting me off. I wheel Aristo toward the river. One Arm's planted on the bank, ten feet from us, his revolver aimed at my head. Aristo skids to a halt.

"I want that colt, boy," One Arm snarls. "Fastest horse I've *ever* seen. Ain't a blue coat be able to catch me when I'm riding him. And it won't take me but a moment to beat the fight out of him. Then he'll stand for the saddle."

Aristo snorts nervously. Trembling racks my limbs.

"You got no way out," One Arm adds. "I can *shoot* you off that horse or you can *get* off. Choose. And I ain't got all day."

I know there's only one choice. If I let One Arm have Aristo, the horse dies a slow, hungry death. And the raiders, why, they'll shoot me like I'm nothing, no matter what I choose.

Dear Jesus, make my dying quick. I aim Aristo toward the oncoming raiders, dig my heels into his sides, and holler, "Run, 'Risto! Run like it's your last race!"

CHAPTER SIXTEEN

Aristo hears the fear in my voice. He rears, front hooves raking the air, then charges toward the circle of raiders.

"Don't shoot that horse!" One Arm hollers.

Several riders rein their mounts in Aristo's path and reaching out, grab at his halter and rope. Other hands clutch my shirt, trying to drag me off the colt.

A bearded face leers at me, then a rifle swings through the air like a club. I raise my arm, the stock hits me square in the elbow, and I pitch off Aristo into a forest of legs. Covering my head, I curl into a ball among the churning hooves.

A cry of alarm rises up. "Blue coats! Blue coats comin'!"

"It's the Yankee cavalry! Head for the river!"

Yelling in confusion, the raiders spur their tired mounts down the bank. A hoof glances off my back. Dirt clods pelt my head. Peering up, I see a wave of blue flowing toward me down the hay field. The soldier riding out front carries an American flag. The others charge with drawn sabers.

"Give me your horse!" One Arm sprints after a raider

who stayed behind to help him. Grabbing the man's leg, he pulls him off the horse, leaps into the saddle, and takes off. With a yelp, the horseless raider crashes after him down the bank and into the water.

I sit up slowly and look around. One Arm and his band are halfway across the river, but there's no sign of Aristo.

The raiders have taken him! I spring to my feet, but my head spins dizzily, and I collapse on the bank. The cavalry swarms around the rocky ledge, the thundering hooves deafening me. The soldiers gallop their horses into the river, pursuing the raiders to the other side where they all vanish into the woods.

The din recedes. I hear shouts from the woods. Then shots.

Closing my eyes, I take shallow breaths. Blood leaks from my wound. My body feels as heavy as a corn sack, and my head drops back against the rock.

I've lost Aristo.

★★★

Warm puffs tickle my neck. My eyelids drift open. Aristo's standing over me. Neck outstretched, he's sniffing my bloody arm, and he looks mighty fine.

Grinning, I cup his muzzle in my hand. "Why, you devil. How'd you get away from those raiders?"

"With a little help," someone says from above me.

I look over my shoulder. A colored Yankee mounted on a cavalry horse stands atop the rocky ledge. The soldier wears a cap and blue uniform, and it takes me a moment to recognize him. "Pa! What're you doing here?" Holding my arm, I try to get to my feet, but my body feels wooden.

"Don't move," Pa warns, "or your ma will have my hide. She and Annabelle are coming down the hill with bandages. Let me dismount and tether these horses and I'll return and see to you."

I fall back against the bank, wondering if I'm dreaming. But minutes later, Pa squats next to me.

I stare at him in amazement. He probes the gash on my arm, but I don't even notice.

"What are you doing here?" I repeat.

"Camp Nelson got word that One Arm and his rebels were back in Woodford County. General Fry ordered the cavalry out to this area."

"How did the cavalry know Master Giles needed help?"

"I pointed them in this direction. I figured the raiders were headed to Woodville for horses. Yankee scouts have been reporting that One Arm's mounts were done for, and I knew he had a score to settle with Mister Giles on account of Tenpenny."

I nod. "You were right. One Arm wanted Penny bad, until he saw Aristo, that is. Good thing the colt is a wild one. You should've seen him attack those raiders! He's still got spirit, Pa. Newcastle didn't beat it out of him."

Pa is gentle as he slides the ripped shirt over my head, but it's stuck to my wound, and I wince when it rips the skin.

"I knew they'd make you a cavalry soldier," I say through gritted teeth.

"Not exactly, Gabriel." Tipping back his cap, he studies my gash. "Wound looks clean."

"You're riding a horse and wearing a uniform, ain't you?"

"Uniform's mine. Horse ain't. Captain Waite called on me to lead his company to Woodville. Company D's all white soldiers."

"Gabriel! Isaac!" Ma's hysterical call rings down the hill.

Pa crooks his lips in a smile. "She's going to baby you, so take it like a man." Standing, he waves. "He's over here, Lucy. The boy's fine."

"Oh, Isaac!" First Ma throws herself into his arms. Then she pulls away and stoops beside me. Annabelle's behind her, a basket of ointments and linen strips looped over her arm.

"Lord, look at all this blood!" Ma gasps.

"Leech takes out more blood than that," Annabelle scoffs, but I can see the concern in her eyes.

"Did the raiders try and get in the house after you, Ma?" I ask. "Are you and Annabelle and Mistress Jane all right?"

Annabelle plucks a huge kitchen knife from the basket. "Wasn't a raider brave enough to tangle with this," she declares, and we all laugh.

Annabelle hands Ma a clean rag and she dabs at my arm. I bite my lip, trying not to cry out.

"Are Jase and Tandy all right?" I ask instead. "Did One Arm get the other horses?"

"Jase made it to Major Wiley's farm and alerted them," Annabelle replies. "Major Wiley and some men came over to help us, but by then the Yankees had arrived and the

141

raiders were scampering off like scared rabbits. Tandy's still lost in the cornfields with some of the horses. Master Giles sent Cato and Renny after them."

"It's a wonder you all made it safely," Ma mutters. "Rebels galloping every which way. Thank the Lord that Pa and the cavalry came in time."

"I bet Captain Conrad's still hidden in the icehouse," I tell Pa. "He got the shakes after the race. I hope he's all right. Maybe you can send someone—

Suddenly, I remember the stallion. "*Patterson!*"

I struggle to stand, but Ma pushes me gently down. "Hush, now, until I bandage this."

"What about Patterson?" Pa asks.

I tell him about hiding the stallion in the pine grove. "Horse must be quaking with worry by now."

"I'll fetch them both. You three all right?"

Ma flaps her hand, and Pa trots off on his horse.

Annabelle hands Ma a small crock. "You were very brave, Gabriel," she says, which is high praise coming from her.

Ma snorts. "Very *foolish*, you mean. Risking your life for Master Giles's horses."

"They ain't just horses, Ma," I say quietly, but I don't expect her to understand.

She sighs as she slathers some smelly stuff on my arm, then bandages the gash with the strips of linen. "There."

Annabelle sets down the basket and gives Ma and me a hand up. My elbow throbs where the rifle cracked it, and I lean against the rock, giving my insides a minute to settle.

Aristo's standing quietly where Pa's tied him to a tree limb. Annabelle helps me up the bank and over to the colt. He nuzzles my hand and I pat his neck, gritty with dust and sweat.

"We made it, 'Risto," I tell him, though I reckon he's feeling as worn and beaten as me.

I untie him, and we start the long hot walk through the hay field, Ma and Annabelle leading the way. We're halfway to the barn when Jase and Tandy come barreling down the hill, mouths flapping. Jase inspects my arm and then launches into the tale of his escape to Major Wiley's. At the same time, Tandy's hanging on my other side, chattering about the chase through the corn.

"We outran 'em, just like you said," Jase exclaims. "Even though Savannah was tuckered from racing Captain, she ran her heart out for me. Daphne's a little sore from trotting barefoot on the road, but we—"

"Let me tell you about Tenpenny," Tandy cuts in with his own boasts. "That horse could outrun his shadow. You were right, Gabriel. Raiders' horses ain't no match for Master's Thoroughbreds."

"Why, you two boys are heroes," Annabelle praises, and they poke out their skinny chests.

By the time we reach the grassy track, the cavalry is coming up the hill behind us. They're escorting a dozen raiders, their hands bound behind them. One Arm ain't with them, but I spot the no-good Rebel who cracked me with his rifle. We stop to watch them pass. In defeat, they look wet and raggedy, not fierce. Ma, Annabelle, Tandy, and Jase cheer their capture, but I'm too spent.

Then Pa rides up from the icehouse leading Captain and Patterson. Captain's mane is laced with dirty cobwebs, but he's walking steadily. Blind Patterson's bobbing his head nervously, but when I stroke his neck, he calms. Neither horse seems too shaken, and my heart swells. We saved them all.

When we reach the barn, Master Giles heartily greets us. He fusses over my arm, then fusses over Aristo, Patterson, and Captain. Newcastle and Flanagan follow behind, clucking their concern. I don't grace them with a look. Any man who would save his own hide without a thought for the horses is no man at all.

"Jase, Tandy, you two boys take Patterson and Captain into the barn," Master says. "See to their care."

"I'll take 'Risto," I say, but Master stops me.

"I want to thank you, Gabriel," he says.

"No need, sir," I murmur.

The soldiers and their prisoners are congregated in front of the barns. An officer leaves the group and walks over to us. Master rushes to shake his hand. "Thank you, Captain Waite, for bringing your company to our rescue."

The captain nods at Pa, who's dismounted and holding his horse. "You need to thank Private Alexander. Our scouts were reporting that One Arm was in Midway. That's where we would have headed except for Private Alexander's insistence."

Pa's expression doesn't change, but Ma and me are just about busting with pride.

"Thank you, Isaac, for bringing the cavalry to our rescue," Master says to Pa. "It appears as well that your son has your courage *and* your love of horses. Cato tells me that if Gabriel hadn't acted so quickly, my Thoroughbreds would have been lost."

This time, Pa and Ma beam. Even Annabelle's grinning at me, and my cheeks heat up.

Newcastle shakes his head. "Too bad you Yanks didn't get One Arm," he says to Captain Waite. "Reckon he'll be back to harass us again?"

"No sir, I believe we captured enough of his band to shut him down in these parts. One Arm's probably making tracks for Missouri. We're taking the captured raiders to Lexington where they'll be jailed and tried in a court of law."

Flanagan bobs his head. "Good. I don't want to face those Rebels ever again."

"You won't need to," Master Giles says sternly. "Newcastle, Flanagan, you two men have ten minutes to pack your belongings. Gabriel proved that he's the jockey for my horses. Captain Waite and his soldiers will escort you to the Midway depot. By tonight I want you on a train north."

Newcastle's face turns bright red. Flanagan's jaw drops, and his eyes flick wildly. "What...why...?" he sputters.

"Shut up, boy," Newcastle snaps, and Flanagan clamps his mouth closed. "You don't need to tell us to leave, *Mister* Giles," Newcastle sneers. "We don't want to work for a boss who chooses a colored man over a white."

He spits in the dirt by Master's shoes. "Racing's a small

world, Giles," he continues. "One day we'll meet again. And you'll be sorry." Casting me an ugly look, he spins on his heels and strides off. The man can't leave too fast for me.

"I should have sent those two packing long ago," Master says. He sighs. "Except once again I am shy a trainer."

I prick up my ears. Master didn't say "shy a jockey."

"Isaac? I sure need you back here," he tells Pa.

"Union army needs him, too," Captain Waite says. "Colonel Sedgwick hopes to organize a colored cavalry. I'm going to need *Corporal* Alexander to help me train men and mounts."

"Oh, Isaac!" Ma gives Pa's arm a squeeze, Master whacks him on the back, and I grin even prouder. *Pa will soon have those stripes!*

Captain Waite bids us a good day, and Pa snaps him a smart salute. We all watch as the captain heads back to his troops.

"Isaac, I owe you mightily for bringing the cavalry to our rescue," Master Giles tells Pa. "I'd like you to have Hero, my saddle horse. Since you'll soon be a mounted soldier, I want you mounted on the best."

"Thank you, sir. I'll gladly take Hero. He's a fine horse. If we do go to war, perhaps he'll keep me from harm."

"Now, Gabriel." Master turns to me. "I believe I owe *you* for saving my horses."

I drop my gaze. "Sir, I don't need thanks for saving the horses. I saved them because…well…" I falter, not sure how to explain. "Because to me they're as important as life itself."

Master Giles nods. "I see. Then perhaps the reward I

should give you is *your* life." He puts his hand on my shoulder. "Gabriel Alexander, you are now a free man."

Did I hear right? I glance up at him, my eyes wide. *Did he say I'm free? As free as Ma and Pa?*

"I'll write up emancipation papers tonight."

Free! I can't speak. The word *free* is ringing too loud in my head.

"However, I would like you to stay and jockey for me, Gabriel," he continues. "You have an incredible gift with horses. I'll pay you a wage as well as part of the purse money."

"The boy will stay," Pa declares. "He is a fine rider, but he needs to keep learning so one day he's the best. And Woodville Farm is a good place to learn."

Ma nods in agreement. "'Sides, he's just a chile who needs to be with his mama," she adds.

"Ma, I ain't no chile," I sputter. "Didn't you hear Master Giles? He said I'm a free *man.*"

"That's right." Master crosses his arms. "These past weeks you've proven that you have a strong voice, Gabriel. Your mother and father want you to stay at Woodville. But I believe you have a say."

My mind whirls. *I'm free. Free to leave Woodville Farm and be what I choose. Free to follow Jackson and be a jockey at Saratoga. Free to follow Pa and be a soldier at Camp Nelson.*

I stare at the circle of them: Ma, Pa, Master, and Annabelle. I hear all their voices telling me about freedom. Then Aristo scratches his face on my shoulder as if reminding me that *he* wants a voice, too.

My head stops whirling. "*Mister* Giles," I say clearly. "Thank you for your offer. For now I'd like to stay at Woodville Farm and jockey your Thoroughbreds." I stroke Aristo's sweaty neck. "I want to stay and train this colt. I aim to build up 'Risto's spirit again, so one day me and him will win such an important race that *both* our names'll be in the *Lexington Observer*."

Mister Giles grins. "A fine decision!" he says. Ma and Pa break into smiles, too, and then they're all chattering to each other.

Sore and exhausted, I limp toward the barn with Aristo, who's just as tuckered. Annabelle falls in beside me.

"I'm glad you're staying," she says shyly. "And I do believe you may be right, Gabriel Alexander. One day, I *will* read your name in the newspaper!"

I glance sideways at her. "That's not the only reason I'm staying, Annabelle. Seems I remember someone told me that freedom ain't just about leaving. It's also about caring. I guess I ain't ready to quit caring 'bout these horses yet."

Annabelle gives me a little smile, and as I walk Aristo into the dark barn, she steps back into the sunlight.

The barn's cool and quiet. I lead the colt past Sympathy, Daphne, and Arrow. Jase is grooming Savannah, and Tandy's rubbing down Captain. Blind Patterson sticks his nose over the stall door, Tenpenny furiously munches hay, and Romance whickers deep in her throat.

Happiness fills me. I'm *free*. Free to be whatever I want and go wherever I choose. Someday soon I'll ride at a famous racetrack like Saratoga. And one day I'll join Pa and the colored soldiers to fight for freedom for *all* slaves.

But for now, I belong right here in this barn.

With my courageous horses.

THE HISTORY BEHIND
GABRIEL'S HORSES

KENTUCKY, 1864

IN THE BEGINNING OF THE CIVIL WAR, Kentucky was considered a "border state," although many Kentuckians owned slaves. During the last two years of the war, Kentucky was under Union control. However, President Lincoln promised Kentucky that he would not free their slaves. This would later change when the Union army became desperate for soldiers.

Toward the end of the war, Union troops took over the town of Lexington, Kentucky. Major buildings became military hospitals, prisons, and barracks. Otherwise, however, life in Kentucky was fairly normal compared to life in most of the Southern states, where fighting was heavy and losses in lives and property were great.

Frances Peter, a young girl living in Lexington during the Civil War, discussed prices in her diary:

Shoes $1.25 to $3.00 a pair
Kid gloves $2.00
A turkey $2.00
One negro man $250.00

AFRICAN AMERICANS, 1864

Because Kentucky was loyal to the Union, the Emancipation Proclamation did not free Kentucky slaves in 1863. Life for young slaves like Gabriel, Tandy, Jase, and Annabelle was not easy. They were considered "property," not people. They had no legal rights. They could be bought and sold at the whim of their owners, or "masters." They could not go to school because it was against the law to educate a slave. Former slave Patsy Mitchner recalled many years later in an interview: "We was not teached to read and write. You better not be caught with no paper in your hand. If you was you got the cowhide."

Young slaves at work

Slaves worked six days a week for no wages. Young children fed the chickens, swept the yards, churned butter, and watched the babies. By thirteen or fourteen they were working as hard as the adults. Silas Jackson, a slave during the Civil War, later wrote that they were "awakened by the blowing of the horn before sunrise…and worked all day until sundown."

Even free African Americans in Kentucky were not totally free. At all times they had to carry "free papers" that identified them by age, name, description, the county where they lived, and details of their emancipation. If a free African

American went out without this document, authorities could throw him in jail.

Like Gabriel's father, free black men often saved up their money to buy their wives' freedom. That way, their children would be born free. Freedom was so important that one African American traded the factory he owned for the freedom of his son.

Early Horse Racing

Many historians have called horse racing America's first national sport. Kentucky horse racing dates back to 1789, when the first racecourse was laid out in The Commons, a parklike area in Lexington, Kentucky. During the Civil War, most racing events were halted. But the racetrack at Lexington where Gabriel raced Tenpenny ran continuously, except in the spring of 1862 when Confederates camped on the racetrack.

Black trainer and jockey at the track

Races were hard on both horse and rider. A race for a three-year-old might be two or three mile-long "heats." Handlers washed and cooled off the horses between heats. Still, by the end of the races, the horses were exhausted and often lame. One newspaper account mentioned a horse that had broken down after 9 1/2 *miles* of racing. Newspaper accounts also described riders fainting from exhaustion and being beaten and battered by the other jockeys.

Early Jockeys

In Kentucky and the South, most of the early trainers and jockeys were slaves like Gabriel, who had been raised with horses. They groomed and exercised horses, cleaned barns and tack, and slept in the stalls. They began to ride in races as early as ten years old.

One of the first great jockeys was Abe Hawkins, a freed slave. Some consider him to be the first African American professional athlete. He was well-respected and valued for his riding skills, and a favorite of newspapers. In 1866, the *New York Times* called Hawkins "that consummate artist in the saddle." His crouched riding style became known as the "American seat" as compared to the upright "English seat."

In the late 1800s there were many talented and winning African American riders and trainers. Ansel Williamson, a slave, was a successful horse trainer for a variety of masters.

Isaac Murphy

Freed after the Civil War, he continued to train horses. He is best known for training Aristides, the winner of the first Kentucky Derby in 1875.

African American Isaac Murphy has been called the greatest jockey in American racing history. He was born in 1860 in Kentucky. He became a jockey at the age of fourteen and won 628 races, including the Kentucky Derby three times.

Camp Nelson, Kentucky

Camp Nelson, where Gabriel's father enlisted, was a Union military camp located south of Lexington. It contained over 300 buildings and covered more than 800 acres. Located within the camp were corrals, a prison, a hospital, a blacksmith shop, a bakery, a laundry, and a Soldiers Home. Set up as a supply depot for Union troops fighting in Tennessee, it also provided and trained horses and mule teams.

Before 1864, the workers who built and ran the camp were generally African Americans who were contrabands (escaped slaves) or those who had been impressed (forced into service) by the army. Recruitment of whites for the Union army began to slow, but the Yankees were still hungry for soldiers. In the Conscriptive Act of February 1864, President Lincoln authorized the use of black troops. Kentucky

Barracks at Camp Nelson

African Americans, free and slave, poured into Camp Nelson to enlist. In return, the slaves were given their freedom. Their masters were paid $300. Freemen like Gabriel's father were given an enlistment fee.

Camp Nelson soon became the third largest recruiting and training center for black soldiers in the country. From November 1864 to April 1865, nearly 5,400 Kentucky slaves enlisted at the camp. Most of the slaves left the farms without permission from their owners, who often took out their anger on the slave's family. Wives and children were beaten or thrown off farms without clothing and food. Many ran away, following their husbands and fathers to Camp Nelson.

Since the women and children were still slaves, the Union army had no legal right to house them at Camp Nelson. Wives and children were repeatedly driven from the camp. On July 6, 1864, General Speed S. Fry ordered that "all negro women and children & men in camp unfit for service [should] be delivered to their owners."

The Real Confederate Guerillas

During the Civil War, there were only a few battles fought in Kentucky. Horsemen in the Bluegrass region continued to breed, raise, and race horses. Wealthy horse owners from the South even brought their horses to Kentucky farms for safety.

Throughout the Civil War, however, Kentucky was plagued by Confederate raiders, often called "guerillas." These men were on the side of the South. Some considered them heroes. Others considered them criminals. Frances Peter wrote in her diary that Rebels "broke open stores and robbed the merchants of boots, shoes and hats." The guerrillas destroyed telegraph offices and supply lines and raided towns and farms, stealing whatever they needed. And what they really needed was horses.

Both the Confederate and Union armies needed horses. Horses and mules pulled supply wagons, cannon, and ambulances to and from the battlegrounds. They also carried cavalry soldiers and officers into battle. The Confederate guerrillas relied on them for raids, fights with Union soldiers, and quick getaways.

One of the most feared Confederate raiders was Sue Mundy, whose real name was Marcellus Jerome Clark. In October 1864, Mundy and his band of guerillas raided Woodburn Farm, one of the largest horse farms in the Lexington area. They stole five valuable horses, including Asteroid, a famous racehorse. The five animals were recovered, but in 1865 Mundy joined with another guerrilla leader, William Clarke Quantrill, and raided the farm again. This time they stole sixteen horses. Asteroid was saved by Ansel Williamson, the farm's trainer, who substituted a different horse. Six of the horses were never found again.

Marcellus Jerome Clark, aka "Sue Mundy"

The notorious Confederate raider John Hunt Morgan rode and fought from Tennessee to Ohio. On July 9, 1864, General Morgan and his band battled a small Union force in Lexington. There, "his men seized hundreds of valuable thoroughbreds, more than enough to mount every rider on a fresh horse." The following lines from the poem "Kentucky Belle," written by Constance Fenimore Woolson (1840–1894), portray the fear evoked by this famous raider:

"I'm sent to warn the neighbors. He isn't a mile behind;

He sweeps up all the horses—every horse that he can find;

Morgan, Morgan the Raider and Morgan's terrible men,

With bowie knives and pistols, are galloping up the glen."

Note: The quote from Patsy Mitchner came from MY FOLKS DON'T WANT ME TO TALK ABOUT SLAVERY: TWENTY-ONE ORAL HISTORIES OF FORMER NORTH CAROLINA SLAVES by Belinda Hurmence (John F. Blair, NC: 1984). The quote from Silas Jackson came from I WAS A SLAVE: THE LIVES OF SLAVE CHILDREN. The orders from Speed S. Fry and the quote about General Morgan came from CAMP NELSON. The quote from Frances Peter came from A UNION WOMAN IN CIVIL WAR KENTUCKY. The verse from "Kentucky Belle" came from *www.civilwarpoetry.org.*

BIBLIOGRAPHICAL NOTE

To RESEARCH AND WRITE GABRIEL'S HORSES, I read more than two hundred books. However, the following sources were crucial:

BOOKS:

Clark, Thomas D. *A History of Kentucky.* J. Stuart Foundation: 1992.

Hollingsworth, Kent. *The Kentucky Thoroughbred.* The University Press of Kentucky: 1976.

Hotaling, Edward. *Great Black Jockeys.* Forum; Rockling, CA: 1999.

Howell, Donna Wyant, ed. *I Was a Slave: The Lives of Slave Children* (Book Five). American Legacy Books, Washington, DC: 1997.

Lucas, Marion B. *A History of Kentucky: From Slavery to Segregation, 1760–1891.* Kentucky Historical Society: 2003.

Mangum, William Preston. "Disaster at Woodburn Farm." The Filson Club History Quarterly, April 1996, Vol. 70, No. 2, pp. 143-185.

Mangum, William Preston. *My Kingdom for a Horse.* Harmony House Publishers, Louisville, KY: 1999.

Marrs, Elijah P. *Life and History of the Reverend Elijah P. Marrs.* Louisville, KY: 1885.

Peter, Frances. *A Union Woman in Civil War Kentucky: The Diary of Frances Peter.* University of Kentucky Press: 2000.

Renau, Lynn S. *Racing Around Kentucky.* Antiques Consultant Inc. Louisville, KY: 1995.

Sears, Richard D. *Camp Nelson, Kentucky.* The University Press of Kentucky: 2002.

WEBSITES:

www.campnelson.org
www.kyhistory.org

THE FOLLOWING BOOKS will help you learn more about slavery and life during the Civil War:

Bial, Raymond. *The Strength of These Arms.* Houghton Mifflin Company, Boston: 1997.

Damon, Duane. *Growing up in the Civil War.* Lerner Publications, Minneapolis: 2003.

Diouf, Sylviane. *Growing up in Slavery.* The Millbrook Press, CN: 2001.

Greene, Meg. *Slave Young, Slave Long.* Lerner Publications Company, NY: 1999.

Hart, Alison. *Fires of Jubilee.* Aladdin Paperbacks, NY: 2003.

Hurmence, Belinda. *Slavery Time When I was Chillun.* GP Putnam's Sons, NY: 1997.

Kalman, Bobbie. *Life on a Plantation*. Crabtree Publishing Company, NY: 1997

Kamma, Anne. *If You Lived When There Was Slavery in America*. Scholastic, Inc., NY: 2004.

Moore, Kay. *If You Lived at the Time of the Civil War*. Scholastic, Inc., NY: 1994.

Union soldiers

ABOUT THE AUTHOR

ALISON HART enjoys writing about history and horses, two of her favorite subjects. "I'd love to go back in time," she says, "and meet people like Gabriel who followed their dreams, no matter what the hardships." Researching GABRIEL'S HORSES took her to the Bluegrass region of Kentucky and its rich Thoroughbred racing and Civil War history. She soon realized that the suspenseful story of Gabriel and his family wouldn't fit in one book. The other titles in the Racing to Freedom trilogy will be GABRIEL'S TRIUMPH and GABRIEL'S JOURNEY.

Ms. Hart, a teacher and author, has written more than twenty books for children and young adults. Many of her titles—including ANNA'S BLIZZARD, an IRA Teacher's Choice and WILLA Finalist, and SHADOW HORSE, an Edgar Nominee—feature horses. Her historical mystery FIRES OF JUBILEE is also set at the time of the Civil War.